THE BULLIED STUDENT WHO CHANGED ALL THE RULES

A NOVEL BY ROBERT M. FISHBEIN

World Publishing and Productions

The Bullied Student Who Changed All the Rules
Copyright ©2024 Robert M. Fishbein

World Publishing and Productions
PO Box 8722, Jupiter, FL 33468
worldpublishingandproductions.com

ISBN: 978-1-957111-28-5
Library of Congress Control Number: 2024908647

Thank you to Mandi Williams for providing the cover design.

Dedication

This story is dedicated to anyone who has ever been bullied. The name "bully" suggests that the offender is in a position of power. But the truth is, often the bully is insecure. If you have been someone's target, I hope this book encourages you to express your feelings to those who care about you. I can tell you from my experiences with students who felt there was no way out—there is always a way out! Expressing yourself will empower you. And that can be your best weapon.

While we are experiencing one of the most challenging times in public education in several areas, bullying has been around for a long time and has not disappeared. Parents, teachers, and all others associated with public and private sector education are struggling.

This book includes a special tribute to the memories of two of the most dedicated educators this author has ever known: my lifetime mentors, Miss "Dot" Dorothy Gould and Dr. William "Mickey" Harvey. Bullies would never stand a chance with these two educational legends.

CONTENTS

Introduction

Has your child looked in the mirror lately? Do they look like someone a bully would pick on? We must teach every child they are strong enough and smart enough to stand up for themselves. Although this is a fictional story, there are far too many actual cases of bullies preying on others, at times seeking an audience and other times acting only out of insecurity, not caring who is watching.

If you are being targeted, know that many resources and people are available to help you overcome bullies. First, you must assess what is attracting bullies to you. Then, get help to overcome the community of rude bullies. I hope Riley's story you are about to read will give you some ideas of just how to do that. You can't let the flies be attracted to you like you're fly paper. You must get help to overcome the community of rude bullies.

Although the school presented in the following pages is fictional, many parts of this story are based on actual events. The topics may be controversial; please know they are derived from one man's experience. Over and over, I have seen teachers who have proven themselves to be prime assets to children who have become successful adults. If you ask any adult to name the people who had a hand in guiding them as they grew up, many names of teachers would come up. As a matter of fact, many would name other members of the teaching staff who also helped them along the way.

We have stretched teachers and other educational personnel way beyond the limits of their capabilities. We can never find enough money to pay them what they are worth. We need to stop telling teachers they work for the government and there's a strict salary scale. Teachers need good salaries and bonuses.

Many individuals make great money working government jobs, and some receive many benefits. For example, look at your chosen representatives: they have shorter working lives, better salaries, and great benefits. Why don't we give the educators a bit less "atta boys and girls" and pay them what they are worth? It's great to be mentioned as a great talent, but it is not enough. Words of affirmation don't pay the bills or offer the teacher a comfortable lifestyle.

Today's students are very much the same as they were years ago, except it has become easier for them to step over the line. Parents today need to be 24/7 parents. Whether one is a single parent, a parent with a partner, or relying on the help of friends or relatives, every child needs someone willing and available to help them through the trials of life 24/7. Many successful people credit that one adult who made a difference in their lives. Yes, being there for a child can be a struggle, and the struggle goes beyond money.

Often, parents expect the school to parent the child—to solve all the problems in the world of growing up. Parents, once the biggest supporters of teachers, have turned on the offense to appease their children. Often, teachers and administrators become targets of parents whose child is unsuccessful. So, instead of creatively teaching and guiding their students, teachers spend precious hours attempting to appease the parents. Teachers need space to teach; they need to be less burdened by school politics and be less on the defensive against attacks that come at them from all angles.

As our story unfolds, we see a child who is bullied even before he enters preschool. His struggle continues through elementary, junior high, and high school. Thanks to some special people, our bullied student takes control and breaks the cycle that has burdened his family for years. Although Riley's situation is fictional, his character's problems reflect many truths prevalent in our school system today. Yet his story stretches from victim to victor as he becomes a role model and mentor despite the continuation of the bullying.

In his early days, Riley doesn't effectively socialize with other kids. Additionally, he has no idea of the current fashion and has his own way of doing things, which annoys other kids—this is just the type of kid bullies often target for their gain. You will see Riley learn, grow, and overcome being bullied, but he also discovers that bullies exist everywhere in life.

Today, equal rights in education are afforded to all. Separating children by their behavior and upbringing is not the way for schools to operate. Learning-disabled children and children with emotional problems need to be included in education. If they have cracker-jack parents who stay the course and demand equal opportunities, new identities for children are on the horizon.

Although there is no formal classification for "bullied" students, they need much attention in school. Sometimes, we put them in a class of the forgotten, but they also need special attention. That is why some classrooms have turned to team teachers—one to teach and one to clarify what is taught and be fully aware of the students' emotional issues.

For Riley, it takes an unlikely classmate, a friend of his dad, and his mom's aggressive behavior to change his course. His dad realizes that Riley needs to have a remake to have a successful life. Riley helps transition by setting his own goals and changing his behavior toward his daily routines. His counselors, although somewhat helpful, are nowhere near as helpful as his own determination to make it all work. He realizes that the accountability of changing starts with him.

Parents know their children better than anyone else. In our story, even two very educated and dedicated parents become the students, while the child becomes their teacher.

Riley learns what is needed to lead an exceptionally productive life and uses his bad experiences of being bullied to teach others. Not until he meets his number one nemesis head-on does he begin his changes. He completely eradicates the need for counseling as he becomes his own counselor. And eventually, what goes around comes around, with the help of a special friend.

The main purpose of this fictional story is to show how one student can separate himself from the bullied population. In no way is this intended to downplay this very serious problem. Bullies exist everywhere. But children and adults should be aware that help is everywhere. When we learn this concept, we will not only become free from bullying but will also make that bully see the error of his ways.

Each state has regulations to fight against bullying. But more importantly, we all need at least one person willing to come alongside us to make a difference in our lives. There are unsung heroes who have helped bullied students become happy, contributing members of our society. This story is about one of them.

Chapter 1

THE BULLYING BEGINS

Riley's days of being bullied began early. When he was in preschool, his neighbor's older cousin, a high schooler named James Jr., claimed the right to control the little kids' playground and develop his prowess. For starters, little Riley Rossey always got his candy and lunch stolen.

"Hey Riley, it's time to make our day," James Jr. and his followers would say.

Riley's crying really did make their day. They would take his lunch, push him to the ground, and chuckle as he lay there, passed by other kids who feigned unawareness so they would not have to get involved. The experience was humiliating for Riley and intimidating for his classmates. To add to his misery, after they took everything, his aggressors made him pass gas before they would walk away in a fit of laughter, finally giving Riley the opportunity to dash into class, often tardy.

As time went on, Riley was recognized as easy prey. His peers learned he had a great mind and discovered that if they took his assignments, they wouldn't have to do them themselves. So, although he did his work regularly, Riley regularly arrived to class empty-handed.

Some would say Riley was a lucky kid because he always had a few extra dollars on him to buy goodies, but that was stolen as well. And if he ever had anything not stolen, he often used it to pay off the bullies in hopes of not getting harassed further that day. But that never really worked.

It isn't surprising that Riley became withdrawn at school and home.

Riley's neighbor and classmate, Jonathan Davis, was James Jr.'s much younger cousin. Jon was supposed to be Riley's friend, but life didn't work out that way. Riley found out the hard way that Jon would never be on his side; instead, Jon, mentored by his cousin, James Jr., became Riley's number one tormentor. Jon seemed to gain strength from being a bully. It must have been in the genes. Jon would feign friendship, offering to push Riley on the swings in the playground. But then he would make him go so high that eventually Riley would fall off and start to cry. There was never a shortage of onlookers who seemed to enjoy watching Jon operate.

The abuse was psychological as well as physical. Riley became accustomed to hearing taunts such as, "Hey Riley, aren't you going to hit back? Because if you're not, I'll keep hitting you."

Besides James Jr., Jon came from a long line of bullies. James Jr. constantly echoed his own father, James Sr., "If you want anything in life, you have to go and get it. Don't worry about who you hurt."

James Sr. himself was the victim of an abusive father, grandfather, and countless others from far down the family tree. He was also known for saying, "Make sure you win at all costs. Losing is for losers, and that is not the Davis family tradition."

Jon's dad, Matt, was serving time for abusing his wife.

Jon's mom, Lisa, was an alcoholic, so she wasn't there for Jon that much. She did take Jon's father to court several times after he beat her silly, knocking out her teeth and breaking her nose. But she always returned to her husband.

Even as the bullying got worse, Riley never told his parents what was going on in school.

Riley's babysitter usually picked him up from school. When he got home, he couldn't wait for snack time. Snack time meant cookies and milk, and he was always hungry. Since he regularly got his lunch money stolen, the cookies and milk became his lunch. The babysitter allowed him his fill due to her own desire to plunge into the sugar.

"There is not enough food in the house," Riley would often tell his mom.

Riley's preschool teachers were unaware of the abuse by Jon and his friends. Who would believe that kids so young could be so bad? Jon was sneaky, and Riley was quiet; he was not about to bring attention to Jon. Their two teachers were new and did not look for the obvious. Ms. Kay was constantly trying to impress her boss and never thought about Riley not eating his lunch or being bullied right before her eyes.

"They never taught us about bullying in college. I would have brought it to the attention of my school director," Ms. Kay said much later. She had a pretty good argument; other teachers have said colleges are more academically oriented than concerned with teaching about student behavior problems. Although professors guide those going into the profession to be excellent academically, many college teachers have never spent a day in schools at the lower levels—either in public or private institutions.

One day, when Riley's mother got home from work, she noticed an empty cookie box on the counter and a gallon of milk and a liter of soda missing from the refrigerator. The babysitter insisted, "I only had one or two cookies and a small glass of milk. I let Riley have the rest since he kept complaining about being hungry."

Mrs. Rossey said, "That box of cookies should have taken four to five days to finish."

"I'm a growing boy," Riley replied to his mom.

His mom wondered if the problem was the babysitter. She'd heard that the young lady also had problems in other homes. So, she hired a new babysitter, but the snack food continued disappearing at an alarming rate. Then, Riley's mom decided to increase the food in his lunchbox—which simply gave Jon and his friends more food to rip off.

Riley was resourceful. He learned to hide money from his weekly allowance in his shoe. Then, he figured out how to sneak into the teachers' lounge to get food from the vending machine. Pretty smart for a preschooler. But Jon and his friends soon caught on and positioned themselves strategically in order to confiscate even those morsels.

Due to a diet consisting mainly of snacks, it didn't take long for Riley to become overweight. Dr. and Mrs. Rossey couldn't understand what was happening, which was unfortunate as Dr. Rossey had also lived through being bullied but seemed to be blind to Riley's predicament. "This must be a normal part of growing up," he thought.

But Mrs. Riley's mom-sense made her wonder if something odd was going on at school—something that was causing her boy to eat alarming amounts of junk at home. She had noticed that Jon didn't come around anymore. When she asked Riley about him, he would just shrug and immediately grab another snack—almost as if the stress of thinking about Jon made him want to eat.

It was not until his parents gave Riley money to buy books at the book fair and he came home without books or money that they finally suspected what was going on. Riley told his parents he had lost the money outside the school, and nobody could find it. What really happened, of course, was that Jon and his friends had stolen the envelope. "Hey, thanks, Riley, for the extra money," they said. "We were able to have a few extra snacks at lunch."

Finally, Riley's mom had enough and decided to take a day off work to get to the bottom of the issue. She scheduled an appointment with the School Director. Her visit was friendly as the School Director and Dr. Rossey were professionally friendly, making it easier for Mrs. Rossey to get around the school and ask questions, but her efforts were not effective.

Mrs. Maggie Whitehurst, the school director, had ample experience with preschool kids, but she still didn't recognize there was a problem. "There are some very aggressive kids here; however, I have spoken to my teachers many times and observed Riley's class. Unfortunately, unless we get several more cameras, we won't be able to see every child and every incident. I don't think any of the kids in Riley's class are causing unusual issues. You mentioned Jonathan Davis, but he has never been a problem. He gets along with all the other students, finishes his work on time, and is always very courteous. I understand he comes from a broken home, but we never see any negative behavior here."

Chapter 2

WHAT GOES AROUND DOES COME AROUND

Later, during his elementary school days, Jon Davis was caught breaking into homes. His cousin, James Jr., was with him, but it seemed he could always weasel out of problems. And he did then, too, telling people he had been there only to discourage Jon. But thanks to people like Riley's father and Jon's victims, Jon was sentenced to a detention center. Cousin James simply told him, "Look, we'll get you out. Since you're young, they won't hold you that long."

Riley's dad, Dr. Richard Rossey, was the principal of their small elementary school and was a prime witness against Jon, as teachers at the school had reported items missing in their classes, and they suspected Jon. Dr. Rossey called Jon's parents several times, but there was never an answer. The police had even gone to the home several times, but Jon's mom seemed disoriented or, a better word—drunk. Jon never told his mom about much of anything, let alone his problems at school. When letters were sent home regarding his grades or behavior, Jon made sure to intercept them. Jon's mom was unaware, and his father was in jail—so he never knew what was going on with anything.

As unaware as the preschool staff had been regarding Jon's behavior, the elementary staff recognized problem after problem, but there was never closure. Jon was sneaky and a master at giving people a look of innocence. Riley's mother could never stand her neighbors, Jon's mother and father. Even before Matt went to jail for abusing Lisa, so many problems had developed in the neighborhood outside of school hours with James and Jon.

Riley's mom had a very strong and protective personality. She confronted James Sr. one day, saying, "All the men in your family—you, your bother, your son, and your nephew—need to learn how to treat others."

James Sr. responded with a surprised look. "Maybe if you and your husband would discipline Riley a little more, we would not have all these problems," he shot back.

"You are all jerks, and everybody knows it."

James Jr.'s mom then chimed in, "You and your husband are constantly provoking James Jr. and Jon. You need to stop blaming everyone for your problems. James Jr. and Jon have never had any problems except in your husband's school. They are not criminals."

Riley's dad testified in court against Jon, saying that Jon was a very bitter kid who was failing school and created many problems, including bullying his son Riley.

Dr. Rossey said, "I tried to contact Jon's mom, but she would never answer or respond to my messages." Jon's mother denied that.

James Jr., who had since graduated from the school district (to the cheers of the staff and administration), and his dad took this very personally and vowed to get back at Dr. Rossey and his family. "Everyone knows that Riley is a clone of you and provokes the kids to harass him. He deserves whatever anyone dishes out to him," said James Sr.

The feud was at a full-blown proportion. One day, while Dr. Rossey was raking leaves in front of his house, he needed a break and went inside for a cup of coffee. When he went back outside, he found his pile of leaves smoking. Dr. Rossey got the hose and put the fire out. However, it was very strange that he saw James Jr. driving by smiling.

On another day, Riley, after a bike ride, left his bike on the grass in front of his house and went inside. When he went outside later, he found one of the tires flat.

The harassment had continued for far too long. It was now time for the Rosseys to install cameras outside the house. But one morning, several of the cameras had been spray painted.

Then, another serious incident followed.

Dr. Rossey and Mrs. Rossey were leaving for church one Sunday morning. When they arrived at their car, Mrs. Rossey noticed the front two tires were flat.

This was strange because Dr. Rossey had gotten an oil change at a nearby service station just the day before, and everything had checked out fine, including the tires. Suspicious, Dr. and Mrs. Rossey decided to clear out their garage to make room for their cars. As they were doing this, Dr. Rossey began to get chest pains. He ignored them, but that night, he had to visit emergency care at the hospital. Thankfully, after a brief stay, he was cleared to go home.

Chapter 3

Elementary School in the Mason School District

Riley and his parents blamed the school and some of the nasty kids in the neighborhood for their bitter and disappointing experience during preschool. You can understand that Riley was leery of entering elementary school, even though his dad was the principal.

The Mason School District, located in a rural area of Pennsylvania, had just over 2200 students enrolled in its best years. The school system had one high school, two junior high schools, and four elementary schools. Many of the school staff lived right in the neighborhood, which led to everyone knowing each other's gossip. Devoted employees agreed that some of their co-workers did not qualify as effective teachers.

It was well-known that the district did not always select the best candidates. Politics ran rampant in this small community through all the local government jobs. Many employees worked in the district because they loved the school schedule—with summers off and the regular closures when there was less than an inch of snow on the ground. They preferred to spend their time hunting, fishing, or boating in the local waters.

Teachers who were hired from towns outside the community did not have the best qualifications, either. The Mason District would not pay for teachers to upgrade their education, nor did they recognize higher degrees for higher pay. Of course, the Rossey family was the exception.

The district was also not proactive with its students. There was very little evaluation of the students post-graduation to determine if they were doing well and if the education they had received was effective. Were they attending post-secondary training? Were they employed out of high school? Did they enter the military?

Dr. Rossey always seemed to be asking, "How do we know if the curriculum we are teaching is working or if we need to make modifications? How can we guide these students successfully if we never assess the outcome?"

But none of this yet mattered to Riley as his first day of elementary school drew near—his hesitation to enter the school stemmed directly from his personal preschool nightmare. To make matters worse, he knew Jon Davis and his followers would be attending the same school. Different location. Same bullies.

The best advice Riley's parents had for him was to give it a try. His dad was very optimistic, but the jury was still out for his mom. Riley was about to find out if his elementary experience would be any different than preschool, knowing the only alternative was to attend the other school across town, where he would not know anyone.

The start of the year was rough. Neither Riley's social skills nor fashion sense had advanced like other kids had. There were clicks, which Riley was not part of, as the kids in the neighborhood stayed away from him, thanks to Jon Davis. And Riley wasn't included by other kids in the school activities either—unless a teacher forced the issue. The roller coaster ride for Riley was on.

Before becoming the elementary principal, Dr. Rossey was the Reading and Math Specialist and was considered one of the top teachers in the school district. He was adept at teaching students with difficulties, including those with learning disabilities. He had worked his way up in the system, beginning as a teacher and then becoming a lead teacher, supervisor, assistant principal, and then a principal. During that time, he also went to night school to complete his doctorate. His dad, Dr. Robert Rossey, had also completed his doctorate in the same program.

Secretly, Richard hoped his son Riley would continue the family tradition. But although Riley was still young, things didn't look promising. Still, Richard remembered that both he and his dad had also been bullied and, at one time, hoped never to see the inside of a school after graduation. The people who had worked in the district for years knew what Robert and Richard had gone through. Things had changed for both him and his dad, so Richard held onto hope they would also turn around for Riley, and he tried to be patient with him. However, bullying had become more dangerous in recent years.

Unfortunately, Richard's dad, Robert, had passed away at an early age and did not reap the full benefits of retirement. Richard missed him and wished he had his guidance to help Riley.

Though the elementary teachers all saw the brilliance in Riley, they also recognized his social issues. Riley was ignored by many students who did not want to bring themselves to his dad's attention. But Jon and his pals couldn't care less about Riley's dad, and they became even more belligerent and conniving than they had been in preschool.

Richard, of course, heard rumblings that Riley was not liked by many of his fellow classmates. He backed off and used his assistant principal as his ears. Heartbreakingly, there were many obvious signs that Riley's school experience was not going well. He didn't know if the name-calling or the fact that many students ignored his son, often leaving him to sit alone in the cafeteria, was worse. And then there were the derogatory remarks written on the bathroom walls. Riley's dress, lack of hygiene, hairstyle, poor complexion, and weight certainly didn't help him. Richard's hope was that Riley would survive just as he and his father had. However, the buildup of resentment was getting noticed throughout the school.

In the neighborhood, Riley became a punching bag. Before Jon got in trouble, the gang made abusing Riley a priority. Every morning, Riley had to pay this cunning group to gain safe passage into school. They were like young criminals, at best. The bathroom and gym locker rooms were not good places to hang out, as these were void of cameras. The kids threw toilet paper at him when they knew he was in the bathroom stall and, of course, wrote nasty words about him on the walls for everyone to read, which most kids just laughed off as a joke. The custodians routinely cleaned the writing, thinking it didn't matter who wrote it or who it was about. Jon was the ringleader. With quite a following of students who wanted to win his approval, Jon was very good at having other kids do his dirty work.

Riley was not well coordinated, so he was never involved in sports. And he didn't join in club activities, feeling he was unwanted. His forte was academics. Riley was a high achiever in math and science; his standardized scores were off the charts for his age. Teachers noticed that he knew as much as many much older students.

Riley's dad continued to be blind to the severity of the bullying issues. And the teachers, who were not really social friends of Dr. Rossey, did not get involved. They felt that as principal, Dr. Rossey should know his kid best and would be completely aware of the situation. Truthfully, their lack of involvement was also partly due to the average person's reluctance to go out of their way to do the right thing. The old saying "No good deed goes unpunished" kept cropping up in many minds. Being branded a snitch in a small community travels quickly and often has a bad ending. So, students and teachers alike kept their mouths shut.

Riley did not have any friends except one classmate, who became a surprisingly good friend. She saw him as a brilliant mind just like she was. Betzy Lejourner was a student who had come to the community from Canada. She was a very pretty girl and had a brilliantly academic mind. It was easy for Betzy to see past all the other concerns and pay attention to Riley's sharp mind. Betzy was very popular and had two brothers who were star athletes. She got involved in sports as a cheerleader since her brothers were also athletes in the local community sports.

Betzy's friendship was a breath of fresh air for Riley, whose appearance left a lot to be desired. He wore clothes that a grandma or the local members of members of the church wouldn't mind but were nowhere near stylish. His hair never looked washed or combed, and his complexion was becoming worse. However, Riley survived his elementary experience—due in no small part to finally having someone to sit next to in the lunchroom.

So after an unrewarding preschool experience and a K-5 journey that was equally unhappy, the next step for Riley was to attend middle school—grades six to eight—which brought a new set of challenges.

You see, although Riley's nemesis, Jon Davis, was now out of the picture, a more prominent bully reemerged. Remember Jon's cousin and mentor, James

Jr? The very James Jr. who taught Jon how to be a bully? Well, he had grown up, physically anyway. "Mr. Davis" now worked in the exact middle school Riley was set to attend.

Chapter 4

James Davis Jr. – How He Wound Up in the School System

We learned how the Davis family operated as a group of bullies, and we will soon find out more about their bullying and how it was dealt with by the Rossey family. But understanding cousin James Jr.'s background is important.

James Davis Jr. was an only child, just like Riley Rossey. His mom, Hilda, worked in the Mason School District as a media specialist. Her husband had gotten her the job through his political connections. James Davis Sr. was an insurance salesman and was active in the town; he was even a member of the city council.

At the school, Hilda was considered a pain in the neck by most standards. She always gave the students a hard time. Most kids thought she would not know a kid even if she bumped into one. She constantly used foul language; one student even reported her to the high school principal for it. Hilda's response was, "That student cursed me out, and I lost control for a minute."

Other students told the administrators she was continuously disrespectful and crass and regularly lied about any and all incidents. They even reported, "Mrs. Davis is on the phone so much she doesn't even notice students going around the safeguards on the computers in the media center to log onto restricted sites."

Hilda Davis came from a very middle-class family. She was a petite woman, while her husband, James Sr., was well over six feet tall. James made it well known he was the man of the house and was always able to get her to shut up and do what she was told. As a child, most people thought James Sr. was an average kid from an average family. How wrong they were! James Sr.—and his mom and dad—had many family secrets.

Hilda's first job for the school system had been as an hourly bus driver. There were quite a few incidents on her bus, requiring her supervisors to schedule two aids to work with her to make up for her shortcomings. Then, she was inconspicuously removed and given a job in the media center at her husband's request, which was fine with her. The change limited her involvement with students—whom she greatly despised. Besides, she no longer had to work the late runs in her new position.

James Sr. was an investor as an insurance salesman who was trying to make his fortune in a few years. He worked every loophole to find a fast track to riches that would provide for his family's necessities and allow him to take an early retirement. He was domineering and would never hesitate to screw his best friend if it meant he would get ahead. He made sure to pass that belief system on to his son, James Jr.

"Man, I don't like working these long hours. It doesn't give me enough time to work out at the gym and play sports with my buddies. I need to find shortcuts to success."

Hilda kept telling him to work in the school system; it would be a good extra part-time job for him.

"Are you kidding me? It'll take forever for me to make any money there. Besides, when I go into the schools, I see so many lazy people who don't look like they care."

James Jr., following the lead of his father, did not believe in hard work and was never a good student academically. He would rather concentrate on sports and dating. Most people didn't consider him a discipline problem because he was so crafty that he never got caught, but his sinister ways were abhorrent to those few who were paying attention. His only real goal was to live an easy life by utilizing every loophole. James Jr. did take it upon himself to show his younger cousin Jon, who was dealing with a lot of family problems, the ropes of life. James told Jon exactly what he had been taught: "It's important to win at everything. Don't worry about who you upset."

Money and security were always at the forefront of the Davis's lives. If they had a motto, it would have been, "Get as much money and power as you possibly can however you can, then retire early." His dad hoped James would get into insurance and investments and ignore trying to land a job with government restraints.

As a young kid and an only child, James had everything handed to him. He was not really rich, but the family played that role, appearing to "keep up with the Joneses." Let's just say he did not know the meaning of the word "struggle." The Davis family had inherited money from Hilda's family and used it to show off more than they could actually afford. James Jr. wore the best clothes and was good-looking. And every girl desired him.

Elementary school was a breeze for James as he perfected his bullying skills, which made many of his peers look up to him. James' elementary school principal was Dr. Richard Rossey, who read James and his family's shams very well. Several teachers accused James of copying his work from others and stealing pencils, pens, and paperclips. James Sr. and Hilda constantly felt like Dr. Rossey singled James out. And maybe he did. Dr. Rossey was sensitive to people lying. He was one of the few people keenly aware of and unwilling to put up with James Jr.'s deception.

Dr. Rossey and the teachers were thrilled when James left and went to the middle school. However, as the story goes, a clone like James was not very far behind.

Chapter 5

James Davis Jr. Starts at the Middle School

James continued the pattern he had developed into his middle school years: charming the girls with smiles and trying to get one over on other guys with webs of deceit. He was a master at using his "friendships" with his "bully followers" and, when trouble arose, always making sure the blame fell on everyone but himself. His athletic prowess continued to evolve, which stirred up the female students even more.

James always had a plan to work his way out of trouble, even though he was part of the group the administrators kept an eye on. He would connivingly tell one story to his friends and then relay an opposite story to the school administrators. It made no difference to him that his friends were caught in the wrong. As James always said, "They aren't really my friends." He was a crackerjack liar. And his mother always stood behind him, right or wrong.

The coaches all loved to have James on their teams. He was an excellent athlete in football and baseball. He spent time in the local gym lifting weights. He would pick a popular, good-looking female to be his girlfriend and then put her under his spell, appearing to be her best friend and soulmate.

The "James Davis Show" continued all through middle school. He charmed Miriam Smith, a brainy classmate, into carrying him through his academic weaknesses. Miriam was one of those intelligent, good-looking female athletes that James lived to bewitch. It took her quite a while—and advice from some teachers and friends—to break free from James' spell and realize he was a total phony.

"I can't believe I wasted so much time with you," she said to James. "We all were mesmerized as you kissed up to teachers and your mother covered your lies, though I'm sure others realized I was doing some of your homework. And I gave you a pass even as I watched you flirting with other girls, steal things like pens, pencils, and books, and treat everyone like you were better than them."

James harshly responded, "Listen, I had no business hanging with you in the first place. You were the worst kisser. Did you bathe every night or skip certain nights? Your parents are strange, and so is your younger sister."

James' attitude infected other kids in the school. And as his influence grew, he used every alliance to his advantage. In such a small town, many people were related, and connections were tight. That came in handy.

One day, James was on his way to school, driving his dad's car with a permit but without a licensed driver. A police officer stopped him for speeding, and when he could not present a valid license, he was given a ticket and a hefty fine.

James smirked, "My dad knows Chief Pollen very well, and he is not going to be happy. "

But this officer was not under James' spell. "I know him pretty well, too," he responded.

"I have been driving this road since I got my permit, and I have never gotten stopped," James said.

"Guess what?" said the officer, "You need to have an adult with you while you're driving. So today is a special day for you."

However, when James and his dad went to court, he walked out without a ticket or a fine—based on a ridiculous story and the fact that his dad was friends with the judge.

"I was bullied by the officer and was stressed out for several days because of the incident."

James' dad verified that story and claimed the incident was his fault as he had an emergency that day and could not be in the car with James.

Another time, James wrote a term paper—well, Miriam wrote a term paper for James. When the teacher questioned James about it, he said, "My mother helped me write it." Although the teacher knew the truth, she also knew that the Davises had a lot of influence in the community and school, so she chose not to pursue the blatant lie.

James' reputation followed him to high school, but he continued to use his craftiness and status as captain of the football and track teams to deceive the masses and keep himself above other students' levels.

Despite multiple accusations from females about his behavior, constantly having others pay for his lunch, and cheating on tests, his new girlfriend, Neese, fell into the same trap Miriam had. Neese was a sweet girl whose own negative self-image left her vulnerable to James, creating a dreadful end to her senior year.

Chapter 6

JAMES GRADUATES HS

After four long years of beating the high school system, James' dad said, "You're graduating from high school, and now it's time to go to a real school. Stop wasting your time with the little people in your world and meet some real people."

James had gotten caught with alcohol at the prom the month before graduation. When questioned, he threw his date under the bus. "Neese supplied the alcohol. I told her it was not a good thing," he told the principal. Despite her innocent plea, Neese was banned from participating in the graduation ceremony and attending the school-wide party. She was crushed, humiliated, and stunned by the deception. James was unaffected.

After the graduation ceremony, James led his friends to his truck, where he had a keg of beer. When one of the teachers keeping watch saw what was going on, he told the students he was calling the principal. James brazenly told the first-year teacher his dad knew the police chief and that his mom and dad were very influential in the community. The teacher said, "Okay, get that truck out of here now." The teacher never reported the incident.

James peeled out of the parking lot, leaving Mason School District in his rearview mirror—never to return. Or so he thought.

Chapter 7

James In College

James and his parents selected a college close to their home for him to further his education. Compared to other schools, John School of Business was considered average and had no strict requirements. Not surprisingly, it was the same school James Sr. had attended, giving him a good enough education to launch him into a mediocre career as an insurance agent and investment banker. Remember, the Davis family's claim to fame was not hard work but getting by on appearances and connections. Accordingly, James Sr. was very active in the alumni association at John, giving James an inside person to turn to if he needed it.

James' first year in college was all about partying. His dad's connections helped him become active in the same fraternity as his dad, through which James got tests and term papers in advance. He had no problem making new friends.

Early in his education, James decided to sell business products and services on campus, just like his dad had. He used the profits for weed and alcohol, which he shared with his favorite friends.

James quickly built an empire in school. He became well-known and established his pattern of skating through the crowd. For example, when clubs and bars required a valid ID for entry, James just walked through with his smile intact. Soon, he started selling tests, class notes, and term papers. Because making friends came easy, getting his hands on class materials and having someone else do his required work was a breeze. Of course, all this ensured James did not get a very good education, but he didn't care about that. He only wanted his diploma and to have a good time while getting it.

One night, while attending a fraternity party, a girl told James in confidence that the party was about to be raided by campus police. She said her dad was on the local police force and had warned her—so she and James left the party quickly, not telling any of their friends about the raid. Later, James said they left because the girl was "hot to trot," and he wanted to bring her back to his dorm. Meanwhile, the kids at the party got busted and had to pay a discipline fine.

James never had a problem getting dates, although he totally disrespected young ladies, especially if they didn't meet his criteria. He would play the nice guy, making girls believe he was interested in them. When he was done flirting and having his fun, he would lie to the girls, telling them that he had just been trying to help his friends get dates. Simply put, he displayed a total lack of respect.

After four years of partying, lying, cheating, earning money off friends, and treating girls poorly, James' vacation was almost over. He was an athlete in two sports but wasn't good enough to make a career of either. He told friends, however, that he had been recruited to more elite programs but wasn't interested. That never happened. The time came for James Jr. to graduate. And the real world was waiting for him.

Chapter 8

James in the Job Market, Dad Does the Work

J ames Jr. got an interview with one of his dad's female friends at a big insurance company. He did not ask too many questions about her or the company and never reviewed the information his dad provided. Not surprisingly, he bombed out at the interview.

He also interviewed for several other jobs—all set up by his father. He finally got an offer via his dad's poker friend. The job had a decent starting salary and good benefits. The main office was in Philadelphia, and there was a good chance that James Jr. could advance or even find a better job after learning more about the insurance business.

It didn't take long, however, before some of the managers realized that despite the extra training and mentors, James was not going to cut it. He did not pay attention to his superiors and looked at his job just as he had school, thinking he could get away with the same tactics he had grown accustomed to. "I'll make my sales quota by charming the customer." But, while charm has its place in the business world, looking good without putting in the hard work and having an extensive knowledge of the product does nothing for the bottom line.

As a last-ditch effort, the company decided to put James on probation and give him a short-range plan for success. Dad came to the rescue. Two customers his dad knew decided to help James Jr. and bought policies from him. Still, not enough money was coming in from those two policies. So, James decided he would make himself popular in the company.

James Jr. became the party planner for employees having birthdays. He spent time ordering lunches for everyone when he should have been on the phone getting sales. Then, he would pick up the lunches, saying he was going out to talk to potential customers. James upgraded his old sneaky habits: he divided the bill when the food came and, for some reason, he always had money left over, which he never returned, instead considering it his own personal bonus.

After discussing his (lack of) progress at several meetings, the company decided it was spending too much time on an ineffective salesperson. And James was let go. Though severance pay carried him through the next two months, James was now out of a job, and he had not taken advantage of the opportunity to learn how to sell.

With one more effort, James Sr. arranged for the company he worked for to hire his son on a thirty-day trial basis. James Sr. was an excellent producer, so his company thought this was a good gamble. James' dad had easily convinced them as he, as we've seen, was a guy who believed in double talk and always got his point across.

That turned out to be a different chapter of the same story. James just was not a salesperson. His father finally realized that business was a losing proposition for his son. "I tried to teach you all the angles, but you just do not listen very well."

Chapter 9

STARTING A CAREER IN EDUCATION...BY ACCIDENT

James couldn't be accountable for any job, it seemed. Contemplating his next move, he called his old neighborhood friend and fellow bully, Jesse Folks, for advice. Jesse seemed to be successful; maybe he would have some ideas. Besides working in a bar part-time, Jesse also worked as a teacher, though in a very poor school district.

Listening to James' dilemma, Jesse considered suggesting that James take up bartending, but then he thought better of it. He knew his old friend; there was no way James would be serious enough to learn how to mix a cocktail or any other mixed drink. But if he couldn't bartend, maybe James had a future in education. His district was always looking for warm bodies.

"Why not come to work at my school?"

"Are you kidding?" James said. "I couldn't wait to get out of college. No more school for me."

"Listen, there aren't many parents who will bother you at this school. When you have a discipline problem, you can send the kid to an administrator who will suspend them for five days and get them out of your hair."

"But I don't know how to teach," James said.

"Perfect, the kids don't want to learn. You can skate through the day by giving them a bunch of worksheets with math, English, and interesting games on them. That keeps them busy for a long time. If parents want their kids to have homework, just give them a pile load of easy work and, the next day, if you get any back, grade them. It's not hard to get certified because nobody wants to teach there. The benefits are great, and you get the summer off. The sports program sucks, so don't worry about having games at the end of the season. If the weather is bad, they close the schools, and you get the day off."

"Ok. You convinced me. I'll give it a try," James said reluctantly.

Chapter 10

THE EDUCATION EXPERIMENT

James was very familiar with the school Jesse suggested—a junior high in a district not far from the Mason District, where James lived and grew up. Since Liberty Middle School was on the other side of town, many teachers there did not know James' background.

Just about the time James got approved for his temporary emergency teaching certificate, the teachers at Liberty had a slowdown; many called in sick to protest the lack of a new contract. This disruption not only caused some of the kids to stay home from school, but it also forced the district to increase the substitute pay rate. James, who had never cared about anyone other than himself, had no problem showing up each day to do very little work and make good money.

Very few activities went on during the slowdown. The gym was open for sports, and the media center showed movies to the kids who made it to school. The cafeteria workers, who were always great to the kids, began giving them extra food since the perishables would not last. The teachers received free lunches, too.

This was a perfect scenario for James. He knew, better than anyone, how to appear busy, give an air of importance, and cater to the bosses. He was also very adamant about the kids behaving. After all, James had a unique expertise in threatening kids, so he was the perfect fit for the sparse staff.

When kids misbehaved, James pulled them aside and threatened to call their parents. Lying to the students made the kids too scared to confront their parents.

As for his own parents, James Sr. and Hilda were particularly friendly with his superintendent, which earned James Jr. brownie points. That made many of his co-workers afraid to say anything nasty about James. Some things never change.

James continued to butter up the administration by helping them with anything they needed. He set up a good network of contacts in and out of the district. To his advantage, Liberty's principal never kept much contact with other schools, and he did not know Dr. Rossey, who was still the elementary principal at the school James had attended.

When the teachers finally returned to work full-time, James became a roving substitute. That meant the school used James wherever they needed him. He also began to work at athletic events, eventually becoming an administrative assistant to the staff.

The principal leaned on James, who used his schmoozing skills to the utmost. He became the go-to for cafeteria duty, bathroom duty, and enforcing rules in the hallways. Students began to visualize him as a person in charge. They feared his threats, which often led to detentions for things the students never even did. He would take kids into the bathroom and push them up against the wall. He used the skills he gained in school to build his little army of snitches. So now he had other kids in the school feeling that you don't mess with Mr. Davis because he carries a lot of power.

It did not take long for James to push his way into the school administrative leadership group. The principal even had James represent him at the out-of-district meetings he did not feel like attending. James made sure to show up in time to get the handouts and the free lunch. Then, he would eat and run, heading home for the day. When he returned to work with the handouts, he took time to make copies and give them to each teacher individually. This kept him out of the classroom for an extended period of time.

Toward the end of the year, the assistant principal began taking time off as she was preparing to retire. So, what did the principal do with James? He used him to handle the discipline issues, of which there were plenty. Of course, James disciplined using his own brand—threatening the kids. And he didn't hesitate to call parents to come and get their child when there was a problem. James' friend Jesse was amazed at how James had pushed his way into the job and become so popular.

With the summer looming, James was looking forward to time off. But before that, the administration used James to help with the end-of-the-school-year activities.

He helped the teachers get kids in groups for senior day, making sure they knew he could remove them from fun activities.

At the prom, which he was invited to by the graduating class who paid for his tuxedo and dinner, James roamed the parking lot, keeping kids from going to their cars to drink alcohol and smoke pot. He was very familiar with that scenario.

He was also recruited to help the regular staff with graduation practice. He ensured the kids knew he could pull them off the stage during the ceremony if they didn't follow directions. And as for the kids he didn't particularly like, James made sure to get even with them during graduation practice. Oh, some parents complained that Mr. Davis threatened students and couldn't care less about the kids in the school, but of course, the school administration always backed him up.

With the school year almost over, the principal decided to retire. And the assistant principal, instead of retiring as everyone suspected, ended up asking for a transfer to the elementary school, which was less stressful. Many supervisors decided it was time to return to the classroom, while others followed the assistant principal and transferred to the elementary school.

Meanwhile, James, the big con artist who used his charm to schmooze the teachers and the staff and was a master at flying under the radar, was loved, or at least accepted, by everybody.

Lo and behold, James' new boss, the just-appointed principal, happened to be good friends with James Sr. Don't be so surprised. The district's latest employee actually got the job, which was not coveted by most, through his political connections. With this fortuitist appointment and the assistant principal position opening still in play, James Jr. began his sly pursuit of the permanent superior position. It wasn't as difficult as you would imagine.

With no one in the system applying for the assistant principal job except one or two over-the-hill teachers looking to increase their pension, the administration began looking outside the district. Meanwhile, James Jr. oozed charisma and charm when he dined with the new principal at his parents' house. And once again, even though James didn't have all the required teaching or administrative certificates, he pushed his way in.

Soon, James was rushing through his certifications, and James' dad was making the necessary phone calls to confirm his son's appointment to the position. James also applied for and got the job as the school's football coach. That was easy as there were no other active candidates.

With the new school year ready to begin, James was excellently positioned. He attended administrative meetings without anyone questioning his credentials. The local, district, and state education offices somehow had no records or transcripts, and most people working in those offices didn't even know James existed.

Still, James began making his mark in his new role. He helped teachers get additional school supplies through his father's networking, saving the district tons of money. That was a big deal for which James won kudos.

Attending college for certification was a breeze. Several adjunct professors gave James a "free pass," so he got his necessary credits quickly. He didn't even need some of the courses he took for credit. He completed a class in constructive discipline, which did not interest him in the least.

James soon decided to run for political office in his very small town, which he won as he was uncontested. The position was easy but put James in the center of the governmental loop. And, according to the town rules, as a town official, James was permitted to be away from the school building two days a month for administrative work. That's called double dipping.

So, the town bully, James Jr., became an assistant principal, coach, and town official. How did he find the time?

James coached sports in the fall, winter, and spring. Don't let this fool you into thinking he suddenly enjoyed being around students. In fact, his attitude toward non-athletic students trying out for a team became increasingly negative; he didn't even try to hide his discrimination against them. And despite his bullying tactics, parents who enjoyed seeing disruptive kids disciplined loved him.

James finally completed his coursework, got his credentials in order, and decided it was time to look for a promotion. When the assistant principal's job opened up in the Latham Middle School, named after James' late godfather, Harry Latham, he was quick to apply.

Mr. Davis Sr. went to work again and, surprise, James Jr. was soon appointed in the Mason School District without an interview or even a job posting. And he got a salary increase to boot.

With his reputation of being a hardass and bully, along with his disdain for kids who are not athletic, it didn't take long for some to complain about Mr. Davis's appointment. But the new school principal, Ms. Schossler, knew she could not make waves.

Chapter 11

Riley and Mr. Davis Collide in Middle School

What an unfortunate coincidence that Riley, having already been bullied for years by James Jr.'s cousin and protégé, was now under the authority of the older Davis cousin, who had just secured a job for himself at Riley's new middle school. It certainly didn't take long for Riley to get overwhelmed in the unfamiliar setting, especially knowing "Mr. Davis" was given charge of student discipline for seventh-grade students.

The Davis family despised Dr. Rossey, Riley's father, even though he was well-respected by others in the Mason School District. First, instead of being the one to hammer the final nail that sentenced Jon to the detention center, they believed Dr. Rossey should have offered to help. In other words, he should've arranged for Jon to avoid any punishment whatsoever. Secondly, they, plain and simple, thought that Dr. Rossey and his whole family were just a bunch of jerks. "The Rosseys have no idea how to build boys into men," said James Sr.

Mr. Davis worked the system. But it was obvious to anyone who knew the backstory: he was stalking Riley, just waiting for the right moment to pounce.

According to his favor for athletes, Mr. Davis ensured they got priority treatment. Despite any trouble an athlete got into, Mr. Davis would never assign a detention that could possibly interfere with a game. Although there were times he couldn't avoid handing out punishments, he was very careful to make sure the timing was right.

One thing that really irked a lot of teachers was Mr. Davis's lack of empathy for challenged students. He despised students who showed any weakness, and he was convinced that challenged students would not boost their self-esteem by sitting on the bench or being ball attendants. When a challenged student had a problem,

Mr. Davis had no sympathy. And when they created a problem due to a medical, psychological, or environmental issue, he punished the student without regard for the circumstance. When parents complained to the principal, Ms. Schossler would say, "Mr. Davis does an excellent job of handling the discipline. It is not going to change my confidence in him. Safety for these children is at the forefront of our decisions."

Teachers at the middle school often had betting pools for sports, thanks to Mr. Davis. In contrast, Dr. Rossey forbade any sort of gambling or betting at the elementary school.

Cheerleaders were always given extra benefits. When Mr. Davis's cheerleading coach was questioned why an obese young lady did not make the cheerleading squad, the coach said she didn't have the skills. A teacher said to others, "That's ridiculous. Mr. Davis made it quite clear he did not want the cheerleaders to be anything but the best-looking students."

Several long-time residents of the district were not surprised that Mr. Davis took that road. People who knew James' father and grandfather knew what nasty people they were. And it was clear in this case that the apple didn't fall far from the tree.

For Riley, achieving high academic scores was his number one priority. His grades and test scores were always high. Getting a "B" to him meant that he did not do a good job with his work. His assignments were always impeccable—thorough, neat, and with the proper heading. And he was working grade levels higher than other students. Riley had a way, though, of making other students look bad. He had not matured in other aspects of the growing-up process, including social dress and getting along with peers. And his parents did not push him in that direction.

The Rosseys attended church regularly. Riley was always there to sing with the choir and perform any other tasks that were needed. He was ridiculed by many of the kids who wanted to be liked by the jocks. They were not quite bullies, but they watched as the bullies operated.

In school, Riley was very good at ticking off kids, many of whom made fun of him constantly. They wrote derogatory comments on his desk and his books—which were always very neatly covered. His brightness worked against him as he often shouted out answers in class, sometimes even before the teacher finished the question. Since he was rarely wrong, that made it worse.

Teachers told his dad how smart he was. Most of them didn't notice—or didn't care—that Riley gave very few fellow students the opportunity to participate in the discussion. The teachers actually made things worse for Riley socially when they commented to the class that other students should be like him. That really added fuel to the fire.

Even when an astute and caring teacher talked to Riley privately, pointing out that some could take his eagerness as arrogance, Riley continued on the same path. Just as in preschool and elementary school, some bullies decided to use Riley's strength for their own benefit. Before Riley handed in an assignment, they would "coax" the answers out of him. If he wouldn't give them, they made sure he knew he would pay after school.

When the teacher asked questions to the class, Riley would wave his hand at the speed of light and shout, "I know!" This brought attention to the other kids.

"You need to put more effort into your work," teachers told their students as they commended Riley.

Some teachers noticed the social stigma and would ask for help to guide Riley. Mr. Davis would listen, then say to himself, "That little idiot is just like his father, making sure that everyone around him looks bad."

And indeed, Riley's father often displayed the same actions in administrative meetings. He often came up with new ideas that created more work than other administrators would like to see. Once, during a staff meeting, James responded to Dr. Rossey, "Is this something you should be doing at home with your own kid? Or something that makes sense school-wide?"

Dr. Rossey responded, "I think you should begin listening more before you make inappropriate statements like that."

Boy, did that set off James. Other administrators just kept their mouths shut. The superintendent kept her mouth shut and said, "Let's move on."

Dr. Rossey was very knowledgeable in his administrative work and had innovative teaching methods in math and English. Riley followed in those footsteps. One day, while Riley was leaving class, he walked up to the teacher's desk to hand in one of his assignments for extra credit. As he did, another student purposefully tripped him, sending him head-first into the wastepaper basket. Riley cut his forehead, broke his glasses, and began bleeding from his head. He fought back the tears, but it was evident he wanted to burst out crying.

The teacher immediately called the nurse, who came quickly to the classroom. Riley's parents were notified, and Riley's dad immediately left his elementary building and was on his way to the school. But Mr. Davis said he was on an important phone call, so he sent one of the counselors to take care of the problem.

Riley was banged up and distraught. "I want my dad," he said loudly enough to be heard by all the kids in the classroom.

Mr. Davis, who had finally arrived, acted like he was concerned, "What happened?"

"He tripped," said one of the students. That seemed to satisfy Mr. Davis.

Riley went to the nurse's office in a wheelchair. When his parents arrived, his dad asked, "What happened?"

The nurse said, "He stumbled and fell."

Riley knew who tripped him but did not want to say anything. He did not want to snitch because he knew that would cause real trouble.

Dr. Rossey decided to visit the teacher in her classroom during her preparation time. He did not inform the front office, however. That really angered Mr. Davis. "Do you think I would walk into your school and go talk to a teacher without notifying you, Dr. Rossey?"

Dr. Rossey gave James the nastiest look as Principal Schossler arrived. Trying to keep the peace, she said, "Dr. Rossey asked for my permission, and I allowed it," which calmed Dr. Rossey down.

Mr. Davis was fuming, however, and said, "Look, I'll make sure everyone involved in this accident is interviewed. If we find this was done purposely, we will punish the students involved appropriately."

Dr. Rossey knew there was more ahead than just the interviews. Riley had to have his glasses fixed, his nose bandaged, and at least three stitches to close the cut on his forehead. Neither he nor Mrs. Rossey believed what happened was an accident. She didn't hide her feelings, "Mr. Davis is such an idiot he won't find out anything. And if he does find out the truth, he won't tell."

Chapter 12

An Honest Student

Later in the day, after the tripping incident, one of the students came to see Mr. Davis in his office. Betzy Lejourner was an honor student and a cheerleader who wanted to tell the true story. "Riley is a very smart and nice kid who is being bullied by so many students in the school. The truth is that John Plasner stuck his foot out and tripped Riley, and I think he was egged on by Casey and Mark."

"Listen," said Mr. Davis, "thank you for coming to me with this information. I will take care of this matter. Do not tell anyone that you came to me. By the way, how are your brothers doing on the football team? "

"Oh, they are great."

"Tell your mom I said hello. You keep those friends of yours on the cheerleading squad happy. Tell them I was asking about them, and if you or your team need anything, let me know."

When Betzy left his office, Mr. Davis said to himself, "That little pain in the butt. Too bad he didn't get hurt worse. His mom is such an idiot, and his dad was lucky the principal intervened."

Later, Riley's mom called the principal and came to the school to visit her friend, who happened to be the school nurse. She wanted to find out what the teacher's report said and what the school was going to do. Riley would not tell his mom the truth because he knew she wouldn't keep quiet; then, he would really get in trouble with the kids. Riley's dad, entrenched in his day at the elementary school, let his wife handle the situation.

When Mrs. Rossey asked the nurse about Mr. Davis, the nurse said, "He talked to several of the kids and concluded that Riley was moving so fast that he tripped on his own feet. Mr. Davis said he would continue to get more facts, and if there were any foul play, he would let her know and punish the students responsible."

Riley never liked missing school, so the next day, he came in with his nose and head bandaged and a black eye. As he walked through the halls, kids were laughing. Many knew what had happened and had even witnessed his crying episode. Some boys harassed him, saying, "Stop making the kids in the class look so bad. You are the teacher's pet, and you're making us all look very bad." Some of the girls who were friends of the bullies repeated the same comments.

During lunch, Riley usually ate alone. But that day, Betzy came to sit next to him. She had long admired Riley, appreciating that he was so academically oriented. While others were leery of tarnishing their own reputation by even being in the vicinity of Riley, that didn't worry Betzy. She knew other students wouldn't say a word because she was a cheerleader. Besides, her brothers were on the football team, and nobody wanted to anger them.

Betzy was a very caring person. Many knew that Riley and Betzy regularly studied together. Their friendship went deep as they often debated issues and challenged each other to solve problems for extra credit. Because they were in advanced classes together, it was natural for them to work together. Some students called them Beauty and The Beast.

Betzy had started cheerleading when she was five years old. She always attended her brothers' sporting events and watched the older cheerleaders, who taught her different cheers. They even let her cheer with them sometimes. Betzy memorized all the cheers. She was a natural.

Some of the kids at the middle school relayed to her brothers that Betzy was hanging out with Riley Rossey, and they took notice, saying, "We don't want our sister hanging out with such a jerk."

But Betzy was independent, bright, and sure of herself. She and Riley talked to each other in several classes. But that did not matter to her two brothers, Tommy and Grant. They wanted her to cool it, or, they said, they would talk to Riley. Betzy screamed at her brothers, "Riley and I study together because so many other kids don't give a darn about school. It is all social to them."

The brothers decided to back off, but they still kept tabs on her. They even went to see their jock pal, Mr. Davis, after school. "Hey, you guys are playing great ball. I'm really proud of you," said Mr. Davis.

"Well, you purchasing those new weights in the weight room was a great help. The guys are all thankful for your support of the sports in the school," said Tommy.

Riley's parents hoped that time would fix their son's problems, but things did not improve. Riley continued to be bullied and ostracized, which his father caught wind of from the teachers. Mr. Davis was no help. It got to the point that Riley thought it would be better to stay home and either be home-schooled or school himself. This enraged Dr. Rossey, who said, "We pay good tax money for you to be educated by the school. We will make this work."

Principal Schossler continued to mentor Mr. Davis; she thought he was doing a fantastic job, though you could say her vision was clouded. Remember, Mr. James Davis Jr. was the son of James Davis Sr., who carried political power in their small town. And Mr. Davis's aunt was on the board of education. It was all in the family. And besides, the sporting teams were doing so well, which made the players' dads and the boosters very happy with Mr. Davis.

Meanwhile, Riley grew more frustrated. He began biting his nails until they bled, not sleeping, and his complexion looked worse than ever.

The Rosseys finally decided to make an appointment with Mr. Davis, although they knew the principal much better. The reality was that Mr. Davis had more direct contact with Riley. Mr. Davis, assuming he was being blamed for all the negative things happening to Riley, said, "People like the Rosseys don't change. They are terrible role models for kids like Riley."

The morning of the appointment, Dr. and Mrs. Rossey entered the school with Riley. But when they arrived, according to Mr. Davis's secretary, their appointment had been moved to an earlier time because of another meeting. Dr. Rossey, who takes pride in being on time for all his appointments, was understandably disturbed. Nonetheless, they had no choice but to leave, allowing Dr. Rossey to get back to his school early.

Seeing Riley come through the front door with his mom and dad carrying a brown bag lunch with his name on it caused the bully group to howl with laughter. To them, Riley looked like a preschooler. This was just more ammunition for the school bullies and their followers. They created a new nickname for Riley, which quickly caught on with all his classmates: Riley the Mama's Baby. Riley never understood where this came from.

The inside stalls of the boys' bathroom had derogatory remarks about Riley all over the walls. Even the rapport he was establishing with Betzy was starting to fade. Her friends tried to convince her that she would be dragged into the mud if she continued to hang around him. When Betzy's name did become attached to Riley's, Betzy's brothers took action.

"You need to stop hanging around that Rossey kid," said Maryanne, Tommy's girlfriend, the high school captain of the cheerleaders. She was hearing remarks daily from the middle school cheerleaders.

Betzy responded, "Riley is one of the brightest, nicest kids I know. He's gotten a bad rap just because he is not popular with the boys. Well, I've got news for you. That Plasner kid is two-faced and one of the biggest followers of the bullies in the school. Without the bullies cheering him on, he's nothing."

All this buzz gave Betzy the kick she needed to confront Riley and tell him what was really happening in the school and why it was happening. Riley was numb to all of Betzy's comments.

Finally, the meeting between Mr. Davis, Riley, and Riley's parents occurred. "I don't want these Rosseys messing up my reputation on handling kids," Davis said to staff members prior to the meeting.

Normally, you would think a "Good morning" or a shake of hands would be the norm at the start of a meeting, but as the Rossey family entered Mr. Davis's office, that did not happen. Dr. Rossey knew that Mr. Davis had connections—he had a direct line to the superintendent, and his dad was on the local planning board and had helped create the district's budget. So Dr. Rossey tried to be professional.

Mr. Davis, who envisioned himself one day becoming the middle school principal and later the high school principal, felt he had the upper hand. He was cocky, knowing he only needed time to get the right people to work for him, and he would be able to retire early with a great pension.

The conference began in a totally useless manner. Nobody brought up any controversial details, and Mr. Davis skirted answering difficult questions.

"Listen," he said to Riley's parents, "I'll talk to some of the students to get them to tone it down. I'm sure they will cooperate, and it'll be much easier for Riley to exist with the other kids."

Sensing a total lack of progress, Mrs. Rossey suddenly exploded. "Look, everyone knows how you got this job and how you treat the kids. 'Bully' is your middle name. You have no respect from the other administrators. You must have something going on in the bedroom with the superintendent to keep her in line. Stop sidestepping the issues and glossing over my son's issues. Do your job and protect ALL your students."

Mr. Davis was infuriated at Mrs. Rossey's outburst. Dr. Rossey turned bright red.

"This conversation is over," said Mr. Davis.

Mrs. Rossey stormed out, followed silently by Dr. Rossey and Riley, who returned to class. Mr. Davis slammed his office door shut behind them. What seemed like a good idea to help the situation had failed.

Later that day, Mr. Davis called Riley down for a private conversation.

"Look, Riley, you need to get your act together. And your mom and dad need to stop covering for you and all your shortcomings. And leave Betzy alone. Your actions are stressing her out and causing her to lose friends. I can't protect you from all the students in the school. After all, your father put quite a target on you by being the elementary school principal."

"You're wrong. Everybody loves my father. My dad says everyone knows you couldn't make it as a teacher, yet you're giving orders to teachers who are excellent. If you were any kind of assistant principal, you would be able to handle this situation."

Mr. Davis got angry at this and said, "Look, you little wimp. Watch the way you talk to me. You're on your own. When you get your butt really kicked, I'll be the first to tell you I told you so. Here's your pass to return to class."

Riley left the office in a very depressed mood and started to plot his plan to avoid his frustration with school. Mr. Davis, "the adult educator," the supposed "leader," had made Riley feel like crap. He thought about where he could hide during the day and not get caught; he checked out classrooms with open doors on his way back to class. Riley developed his plan, which he would implement the following day.

Chapter 13

Riley's Special Friend

After spending days cutting classes and avoiding being seen, Riley found the perfect place to hide—the boiler room, which was always left unlocked. He would go there after getting the class assignments from Betzy. She tried to talk him out of cutting classes, but he claimed, "This is the only way that I can survive and not feel worse than I do."

One day, out of nowhere, a tall man with a hunter's hat, jeans, and a flannel shirt walked in and sat next to him. Riley did not know who the man was, but the man knew Riley immediately.

"Hey, you live over on Woodbine Street, right?"

Riley shook his head.

The man, whom Riley would soon find out was Mr. Alfred, continued, "Your dad is Dr. Rossey? Listen, I worked for your dad when I was first employed in the district. He was the best boss I have ever had."

Mr. Alfred was a man of decorated titles: he was on the Board of Education in a nearby district, a volunteer fireman, a police auxiliary member, and a member of the county's veteran society. He was a genius at fixing things in the various schools, saving the district thousands of dollars. Mr. Alfred's phone rang while he was talking to Riley. He answered and quickly told the caller that he was busy in the boiler room and may be there for a little while.

"So, Riley, I heard a little bit of what was going down with you, and it sounds like you can use a friend. Before you start talking, let me run a few stories by you and tell you how my group handles harassment."

"You see, we are considered the lowest of the employees here at the school. Many men on my staff were not the sharpest students in school, but they had the remarkable ability to troubleshoot and solve building problems, saving the district a load of money and aggravation."

Mr. Alfred made it seem like he was in touch with a power beyond the norm. "Listen, Riley, my men have been laughed at a lot behind their backs, but they have learned how to handle it."

"My crew recognizes when people kiss up to them when they need them and ignore them as nonexistent when they don't. You see, Riley, what happens when we are not treated with respect is we put the work orders of those people to the very bottom of our to-do list."

"A prime example of a jerk is your Mr. Davis. He thinks we are just a bunch of uneducated guys with small minds. But, when he needs something done, he acts like we are kings. Then, as soon as we make him look good by fixing his problems, he takes the credit and runs, leaving us covered in the dust from his shoes."

Mr. Alfred continued, "Just be careful what you say and how you say it. Good people recognize good people. Those who matter will get your drift without a word coming out of your mouth. You keep acing the tests and getting the best class scores. I know an angel I'm going to consult, and trust me, you will see your life turn around. Don't ask questions. Don't make comments. And don't wonder how this is happening. But do come to the custodians' office whenever you need to. Talk to the guys and have a cup of coffee with us. Meanwhile, don't tell anyone about our conversation. You know where the maintenance office is located. My guys will give you advice about how to handle the bullies—including Mr. Davis, the biggest bully of them all."

Riley did not know what to think or what to say. He actually had a place to hang out. So he did. He began by making small talk with some of Mr. Alfred's staff, and slowly, he learned to trust them.

"Wow, you guys are awesome," Riley told them one day. "You probably have as much, if not more, common sense than some teachers." Well, this only led to the men telling Riley more of their stories.

Riley learned that most of the maintenance staff served in the military and were excellent at repairing anything. Many even built their own houses. They also had exciting hobbies, like fishing and hunting, were very active in local community activities, and many of them had a strong faith.

While most kids in school socialize with their peers, Riley was socializing with people in their 40s and 50s. He learned from their vast life experiences and even saw pictures of medals they received while in the service.

So why were these great men working as custodians in the local school district? Mr. Alfred answered that question. "We all have great skills and do side work. We need the medical benefits and pensions we don't have. Plus, we all enjoy working around young kids like you."

One day, while Mr. Davis was doing his rounds, he came by the custodians' office. For a rare moment, he entered the room only to find Riley sitting with staff and having coffee. "What is one of my students doing in here?" asked Mr. Davis sternly.

Mr. Alfred, who does not like disrespectful people, said, "Well, it's before school hours, and we all like Riley."

"You custodians get off your coffee break and get to work. And you, Mr. Rossey, go hang out with the other kids until the bell rings to go to class. That's if you can find a person who likes to be with you. Let me know."

Mr. Alfred looked at Riley and told him to listen to Mr. Davis, so Riley left the room. No one messed with Mr. Alfred without consequences, and Mr. Davis had gone over the line. Mr. Alfred, besides all his other strengths, had served the country in a foreign war and was a third-generation resident of the town.

After Riley left, Mr. Alfred told Mr. Davis privately, "The next time you come into this office, you need to knock and excuse yourself, just like I would if I entered your office. If you can't do that, don't come in." The staff started getting their tools for their work orders and headed out the door. They knew Mr. Alfred was steaming mad. Mr. Davis ran out quickly as he could see the smoke coming from Mr. Alfred's nose.

At the end of the day, Mr. Alfred received a memo from Mr. Davis. He read it in front of his men, then ripped it to shreds and threw it in an envelope with "Low Priority" written across it. He put the envelope next to another envelope labeled "High Priority," which could have just as clearly been marked "Projects for the People We Respect."

Chapter 14

Mr. Alfred's Influence

Mr. Davis consulted Superintendent Heck about the Riley Rossey problem—specifically about Riley hanging out in the maintenance office. Everyone knew Mrs. Heck was a friend of James Sr., Mr. Davis's father. Everyone also suspected the two school employees had loyalties to each other that ran deeper than a "professional" level. Still, Mrs. Heck was the superintendent, so it was not off-base for Mr. Davis to consult her. However, although she had finished her master's program and held the proper licenses, Mrs. Heck was not very experienced with middle school students.

But when Mr. Davis, who thought he had curtailed the problem, saw Riley leaving the maintenance office smiling, he became enraged and set an appointment with Mr. Alfred.

Mr. Davis, being sly and devious, hid a recorder in his office and requested that a specific fellow staff member, who had no backbone of his own and regularly delegated to the assistant principal, be present. Knowing what a weasel and sneak Mr. Davis was, Mr. Alfred intentionally cornered Mr. Davis alone after school in the building the day before the scheduled meeting.

"I will be in your office tomorrow. But rest assured, you have opened a box you should have never opened, and you will more than regret it."

Shaken by the threat, the next day, Mr. Davis brought in one of his counselors to be a witness during their conference. Mr. Davis had a prepared speech with his usual antics.

Mr. Alfred replied simply, "You're right, sir. I was wrong. I will tell Riley he cannot come into our office during the school day without your permission." Then he went on to praise Mr. Davis, who, in shock, ended the meeting abruptly.

The next day, while driving to work, Mr. Davis was stopped by a police officer he didn't know who gave him several violations: speeding, driving without his license, not wearing a seat belt (which he took off while reaching for his registration), and having a brake light out—something Mr. Davis was not even aware of.

Of course, he arrived late to school, and when he went into his office, the temperature was nearly 90 degrees. He called Mr. Alfred, who said he would send someone immediately to check the thermostat. "Immediately" turned into forty minutes. Finally, Mr. Davis was forced out of his comfort zone—he went to the custodian's room and knocked on the door.

Mr. Alfred opened the door. "What can I do for you, Jim?"

"What happened with the room temperature?"

"We had to order a thermostat for you. It will be here this afternoon."

Lo and behold, the thermostat did not arrive that afternoon. Mr. Davis had to deal with the sweltering heat in his office the rest of that day and even the next day.

The bullying didn't stop for Riley. He was in the lunch line when John Plasner once again tripped him. Riley's tray went flying, spraying milk all over the bully's face, which made the other kids laugh. Then, Plasner and two of his cohorts slipped in the milk, ending up on the floor. With milk all over his clothes, Plasner screamed, "You jerk! Riley, you and me after school." Riley just stood there in disbelief. He didn't do anything. But John and his buddies were embarrassed.

As Riley headed to class, several students shouted, "Good job, Rossey. You sure showed Plasner and his boys what they deserved." And when Riley went to his afternoon class, other students started slapping him five.

Meanwhile, John Plasner's mom arrived at school to bring him clean clothes, even as the word got out that Riley and John were going to fight in the park near the school.

When school let out, students showed up, waiting for a fight to start, but Riley didn't show up. Plasner, standing in front of the crowd telling everyone he was going to beat the crap out of "that wimp, Rossey," suddenly looked up and saw his mom and dad in front of him.

"What are you doing here?" he stammered.

"We were told by a staff member that you were in danger of being jumped by a gang of kids, so we came here quickly."

Next came a police car with sirens blasting, causing the gang of kids to retreat. Dumbfounded, John was led away by his mom and dad, who took him home.

"By the way," John's dad said, "I got a call from my fishing buddy, Archie Alfred, who tells me you're a wise guy in school. You better get rid of that attitude quick."

The kids looking on began chuckling, wondering just how much of a bully John Plasner really was.

That night, Mr. Alfred stopped by the Rosseys' house. "Rich, how are you?"

"How are you, Archie?" said Dr. Rossey. "It's so good to see you. What brings you here?"

"Well, Riley and I have been talking and have become sort of pals at the middle school. I wondered if Sam, Henry, and I could take him fishing with us this weekend?"

"Sure," said Dr. Rossey. "I never knew he had an interest."

"Yup, we got to talking, and I mentioned my boat. I told him I'd see about taking him out sometime. Since you are okay with it, I'll pick him up, and we will have breakfast and lunch together."

Just then, Riley came in and smiled when he saw Mr. Alfred. "Dad, Mr. Alfred is so awesome."

"Yes, I know. I wish he still worked in my building."

Mr. Alfred looked at Riley and said, "When you are in the cafeteria tomorrow, look Plasner dead in his face and drink your milk right in front of him. I guarantee the kids around him will laugh."

That night, Mr. Davis got ready for bed and a good night's sleep. But during the night, he was in dreamland when suddenly a message came to him: "Beware of the Rosseys, Mr. Alfred, and their secret power. Make sure they stay safe." The message kept repeating so many times that it woke him up in a deep sweat. James remembered the words.

"What the heck was that, and where did it come from?" he thought to himself. Between all that was happening with Mr. Alfred and now having this dream, Mr. Davis couldn't stop wondering what was happening. "Ah, forget it. I'm not going to let an old fisherman and the Rosseys change anything in my life."

The next day, Mr. Davis called several students into his office and said, "You three are suspended for harassment of Riley Rossey. If it happens again, you will be barred from all activities for the rest of the year." The students were totally shocked. They all questioned where the information came from. Mr. Davis was mum.

Their parents were not notified, and there was outrage as two of the three were "A" parents. Superintendent Heck was not very happy. She called James and said, "What are you doing? How could you put me in such an awkward position?"

James said, "I was trying to do what was right. I didn't know that these kids had A parents."

James began to think about his dream the night before. "Don't tell me that the Rosseys and the janitor are running my life, no way."

The rumor in the school was that Dr. Rossey told Mr. Davis to suspend the students. "My son is a good kid and very popular in school and in the community. This tarnishes his perfect record," said Mrs. Stonehill, one of the parents. "Michael does not pick on any students."

Little did she know that her son Michael, though an honor student, was one of Plasner's henchmen who helped him by being in charge of future bullying activities.

"The Rosseys are causing big problems. I better handle this myself," Heck said to James.

Then, to the parents of the three suspended students, Heck said, "The Rosseys like to use their name and blame these situations on others. Mr. Davis has always done a good job but made a mistake. He is willing to rescind the suspensions on the three boys."

Then Mrs. Heck made an appointment with the Rosseys. After greeting them, she told Dr. and Mrs. Rossey that Riley was causing problems, and the Board of Education wanted this to go away.

"It'll wind up being very ugly if it continues. People will start taking sides. He's your kid, and you need to teach him what it takes to make it in middle school. You pampered your kid through elementary school and ticked off a lot of people. I know he's getting great grades, but he is despised. He lacks the social skills to mingle with other kids. I've seen your kid in the community; he's a nice kid. He deserves a good education and not to be bullied. But in situations like this, poor parenting is to blame as much as other kids."

This, of course, enraged Mrs. Rossey, who responded with an R-rated rampage that was heard throughout the office.

A bit more level-headed, Dr. Rossey supported his wife's outrage. "We'll do an investigation on Mr. Davis and why you support that idiot so much. You have no idea what you've started. Everyone in the district knows how you operate and how you got this job. Davis's aunt covers his butt, as does that father of his. If you want to address bullying in this district, start with the Davis family. You and Davis do not advocate for kids unless they are athletic stars, then you kiss their butts. Every kid deserves a fair education despite any problems they are encountering. Riley is an eager learner. You were a teacher once. Don't you remember why you became a teacher?" Then he added, "I guess we have to take this to the Board."

Mrs. Heck replied," Don't do that. That will only make you look bad."

"You mean to tell me that if I tell the truth, it will reflect poorly on *me*?"

"I suggest you put your son in a private school where there is a smaller number of students."

"Screw you, Heck. My kid is staying right here, and we will win this battle," proclaimed Mrs. Rossey.

That night, the police stopped Mrs. Heck as she was speeding down the street. She waited as the officer decided to check out her credentials. It seemed Mrs. Heck's record indicated that she did not pay a parking ticket in her last school district, did not renew her license, had a brake light out, and her car had somehow come up as leaving the scene of an accident in her mother's neighborhood two years ago. Mrs. Heck became very nervous and began fumbling to find her insurance card and registration.

Later, when Riley learned about this incident, he asked his parents, "Mr. Alfred didn't know about Mrs. Heck being stopped by the police, did he?"

Dr. Rossey just smiled.

Chapter 15

Bad Luck for the Davis Family

When report cards came out, it was no surprise to anyone that Riley got all As, just as he always had. Despite missing class regularly, he had developed a system of getting and turning in his work through Betzy. But his problems were not yet over. Neither were Mr. Davis's.

Once again, Mr. Davis was stopped by the police, this time for not stopping at a stop sign. As the officer gave the summons, he said, "We'll keep this low-key so the students don't find out we've had to stop you on several occasions. That's not a good look for a role model." He pleaded with the officer to let him off, but to no avail. It seems like Mr. Alfred and Officer Russell were family.

Not only were the traffic tickets stacking up for Mr. Davis, but things grew more and more tense at school as the school board meeting drew closer and the Riley Rossey situation was sure to be a topic of discussion.

Superintendent Heck knew that somehow Mr. Alfred was involved in all the difficulties going on, but she couldn't pinpoint how.

Mr. Davis continued to do everything to save himself. "That damn Rossey kid started this whole thing, and his old man is to blame as well." He even started the rumor that it was Dr. Rossey who made him suspend those students. Meanwhile, Principal Schossler, who only had a couple more years to work and didn't want to make—or deal with—waves, assured the Rosseys she would watch out for Riley.

When the board meeting arrived, the Rosseys, Superintendent Heck, Principal Schossler, Mr. Davis, and Mr. Alfred were all present, along with several teaching staff, maintenance workers, and members of the community.

It didn't take long for the board to hear from Mrs. Rossey.

"Good evening, ladies and gentlemen. First, let me advise you that we have several adult bullies at tonight's meeting."

This statement surprised everyone. Faces immediately started cringing, especially when three police officers from the community entered the meeting dressed in full uniform.

Mrs. Rossey continued, "The bullying this school faces with students also occurs within the administrative staff."

At that point, Mrs. Heck stopped Mrs. Rossey because several press members were present. "I recommend that the board go into private sessions before we hear any more of this." The president of the board asked for a vote, and the board voted in favor. Then Mrs. Heck continued, "Mrs. Rossey, with all due respect, we would like to discuss some matters that are very important. I assure you, we will give you the opportunity to continue once we reconvene."

Many of the people in the packed house sat in surprise as the board members gathered their belongings and retreated to a private room.

One parent said, "I hope they are going to address Mr. Davis and Mrs. Heck—the two major problems we are facing."

Others said, "It's that damn Rossey kid that's causing all these issues."

The Rossey family left the area so as not to have confrontations. Mr. Alfred left the area as well. All of a sudden, one board member returned and asked the Rosseys to join the private session.

"Wait," said Dr. Rossey. "We want Mr. Alfred to come with us. Otherwise, the answer is no."

While the board consulted with their attorney, Dr. and Mrs. Rossey and Mr. Alfred entered the private room where the board members and Mrs. Heck were sitting around a large table.

Before anyone could speak, Mr. Alfred respectfully asked permission to bring Lieutenant Ron Colbert into the room. "Lieutenant Colbert would like to present some important information to the board members." Mr. Alfred had so much influence he rarely got turned down.

After he entered the room and was given the floor, Lieutenant Colbert began, "Thank you, members of the board. While hearing about the controversy over what is happening in the district, I'd like to present information given to me by Mrs. Heck's last district of record."

The board attorney objected, "This private hearing has nothing to do with Mrs. Heck. It is the Rosseys that we are concerned with."

"As the superintendent who has inserted herself into the Rossey situation, we would be negligent not to address Mrs. Heck's role. And based on public law, when addressing the role of the superintendent, we must allow the press access to this report, which may explain Mrs. Heck's behavior in the district."

The board began a back-and-forth match. Meanwhile, Mrs. Heck was sweating it out, but she had no choice but to sit and hope for the best.

Lieutenant Colbert continued, "Mr. Chairman, it seems Mr. Davis Sr. may have had some close encounters with Mrs. Heck."

Mrs. Heck, no longer able to contain herself, chimed in. "I can explain very easily. I was purchasing some investments from Mr. Davis, and we met in a restaurant. Mrs. Davis was invited but was sick at the time, and Mr. Heck was out of town."

"That may be true," says the officer, "but your meeting is reported to have gone beyond the restaurant. We have a positive ID that Mrs. Heck and Mr. Davis signed into the Commerce Hotel twenty miles away as Mr. and Mrs. Patton."

At that point, Mrs. Heck slammed her hand on the table. "That is so ridiculous!"

"This inappropriate affair with James Davis Sr. certainly sheds light on why James Davis Jr., who is woefully unqualified, was hired by Superintendent Heck for the position of assistant principal."

At that, Mrs. Heck stormed out of the room and out the back door of the building.

After some grumbling among the board, the president returned to the main room and announced to all those present, "Due to an emergency, this meeting is adjourned until further notice." The crowd was stunned.

The following days, as you can imagine, were full of repercussions.

Mr. Davis Sr. and Mrs. Davis got into a massive fight after Mrs. Davis learned of the incident. Never one to face his own actions, Mr. Davis Sr. took off on a solo vacation.

Superintendent Heck applied for medical leave, claiming mental stress. Then she opened lawsuits against the district, the Rosseys, Mr. Alfred, the police department, and everyone else she could think of.

Mr. Heck went out of town, but guess what? He filed for divorce when he heard about the claim. He had always suspected that Davis Sr. and his wife were involved in an affair.

And the district, attempting to get past the bombshell, appointed Mrs. Schossler the acting superintendent. Then, without another option available, they put Mr. Davis Jr. on strict warning but appointed him as acting principal of the middle school.

The last thing on anybody's mind was the Rosseys. Mr. Alfred struck again.

Chapter 16

Mr. Davis Jr. Is Shaking in His Boots

Mr. Davis couldn't wait for the school year to be over, knowing that Riley Rossey would be headed for high school.

Riley had proven his academic ability beyond any level ever seen, basically teaching himself the eighth-grade curriculum. For him, the rest of the school year was a breeze as the parents, teachers, and students had become keenly aware of what all that had happened.

Wanting to keep his nose clean, Mr. Davis worked to ensure that Riley had no problems. But he was quietly fuming and plotting his future moves against the Rosseys. "That Rossey is responsible for this mess; I'm not done with him," he promised himself.

Finally understanding Mr. Alfred's power, Mr. Davis avoided Mr. Alfred and his staff like the plague, which allowed Riley to have lunch and snacks with the maintenance men daily. Rily loved telling them about all he was learning, especially since he had been able to return to class. And they were always eager to listen to him.

Mr. Alfred told Riley, "You know what? You would be a good teacher."

Riley laughed and asked, "Am I allowed to curse in here?"

"Yup," said Mr. Alfred.

"Well then, hell, no!" Riley responded.

Mr. Alfred was waiting for Mr. Davis to make a move. Better said, he actually hoped he would. When Mr. Davis sent memos, they went right into the garbage as a paper basketball.

The end of the year finally arrived. During the graduation ceremonies, Riley's teachers gave him many awards for his tutoring work and club activities. Mr.

Davis was smart enough to smile and clap for Riley. The board members on the stage were happy there was peace, at least on that night.

Mr. Alfred and his entire district staff were also at the ceremony, clapping away. They were given the time off with pay to attend. Mr. Alfred presented Riley with a special award—The Maintenance Staff's Student of the Year. The guys stood up and cheered. Riley was teary-eyed, as were his parents and many others in the audience.

Chapter 17

High School Preparations

The end of Riley's middle school experience brought changes for many. At the high school, there would be students from both junior high schools, putting Riley and his classmates among many students they didn't yet know. He and Betzy vowed to keep in contact with each other. And Mr. Alfred? Well, he asked for a transfer to the high school, knowing it would give him the opportunity to continue seeing and monitoring the progress of his friend, Riley.

Mr. and Mrs. Davis Sr. officially separated, and Mrs. Davis disappeared from sight. Mrs. Heck, who was originally from Texas, moved back to her hometown while Mr. Heck remained, now living alone. Dr. and Mrs. Rossey had high hopes for Riley's future, whose summer break became one of the most important times of his life.

And Riley got away from Mr. Davis Jr, who remained the acting principal at the middle school. (Of course, Mr. Davis was elated that Mr. Alfred had asked for a transfer to the high school supervisor position.)

Betzy quickly became co-captain of the high school cheerleading squad, which practiced over the summer. The cheerleading coach, Mrs. Vicky, warned Betzy that hanging out with Riley would be a negative for her in high school, possibly causing her issues with the other kids. Betzy stood her ground, "Both my brothers are here at the high school and will look out for me. Plus, I can take care of myself very well."

The summer was a transformation period for Riley. He continued to be very friendly with all of Mr. Alfred's staff, even becoming a seasoned fisherman from their regular outings.

Several other high school kids hung around this group of adults, and they all got to know each other much better out of school. Mr. Alfred also provided employment for the kids—assigning them as heavy-duty summer workers at the high school, where there was much to be done. Riley would wear work clothes that were gratifyingly filthy and sweaty by the end of each day.

The first few days of this physical labor made Riley tired but happy. After that, he felt good and began building muscles and losing weight. The team continued to prepare Riley for high school, helping him understand in advance what he needed to know and what would be helpful for him to change. For Riley, this was all new. But he was beginning to get it.

Besides fishing and working, the boys did some bow and arrow hunting and regularly went to the weight room, which was also a new experience for Riley. The group even showed Riley what to eat to maintain strength and look good.

Mr. Alfred explained that being in high school would be like being a part-time actor and part-time student, and knowing how to present yourself to teachers and students was of utmost importance.

"Eating in the cafeteria is also an art," Mr. Alfred explained to Riley. You don't want the kids to believe that you're different because you're not. What is important is consistency, consistency, and more consistency. That's a critical word for you to remember. Don't change who you are, instead, change how you handle things. That's very important."

Mr. Alfred's Boys, as the group came to be known, really took a liking to Riley and shared with him some secrets about how to deal with women. That's when he told them he was friendly with Betzy. This turned out good for them to know as a couple of them played football and knew Betzy's two brothers well.

As summer moved along, Riley began feeling good about himself. He had lost weight and gotten a more stylish haircut, new contact lenses, and all the appropriate notebooks and book bags. He was ready to go.

One night, Mr. Alfred took the boys out to eat. They had a blast, taking Mr. Alfred's wallet for a ride. The old Riley had become a new Riley.

As Mr. Alfred started his new job at the high school, he spoke to the principal, Mr. Toby, telling him about Riley.

"I know all about the middle school," said Mr. Toby. "And I am very familiar with James Davis. Riley will not have the same problems here, I assure you. Rich Rossey and I have already spoken, and he trusts my judgment just like I have always trusted his."

Mr. Alfred was intent on building a great team at his new school. Not only was the high school maintenance crew gifted at doing their job, but they, along with Mr. Alfred's Boys, were the eyes and ears of the school, watching out for those who were bullied and mistreated, including Riley Rossey.

So Riley was set up for success in high school.

However, there was a new issue lurking. Riley's former neighbor, now not-so-little Jonathan Davis, who had spent time away in a facility for breaking into homes and then attended the other middle school in Mason—Riley's original bully and cousin to the infamous James Davis Jr.—would soon be back in the picture.

Chapter 18

A New Beginning

Riley's freshman year was off to a great start. His body and mind were strong. And with the help of Team Alfred, Riley became more comfortable than ever and was enjoying school.

Principal Toby was a very good man, as were his assistants. The school was a feeder for another middle school, and because the classes were tiered and Riley was in the highest accelerated classes, there were many students who did not know him. Besides, because of his fresh haircut, fashionable clothes, and a body that looked brand new, Riley was nearly unrecognizable.

Riley was a wiz in his accelerated classes, with his high IQ immediately helping him. He also registered for two of his favorite non-track classes: auto shop and computer repair, which he thoroughly enjoyed. And though challenging, he most looked forward to his math and English classes. Probably because Betzy was in both.

Riley's lunch schedule allowed him to eat in the cafeteria with some upper classroom friends from the summer who introduced him to some of their friends.

With his newfound strength, even gym class was very comfortable. That is, until Riley discovered that Jon Davis and some of his buddies were in the same class. Suddenly, his elementary and middle school issues threatened to resurface. With none of his upper-level friends around, Riley's vulnerability began to return.

One particular day, they were playing kickball when Riley got a ball kicked right at his face. He held his ground; his face was stoic as some of Jon's friends observed his reaction. Riley did not go into a corner and hide; he just stepped aside to make sure his contacts were intact. Then he returned to the game. Several of his new mates slapped him a high-five, and the game went on.

After the class, Riley headed down the hallway to his next class, only to be circled by two students who asked why he was talking about them. Realizing it was a setup, Riley tried to move on but was stopped in his tracks.

Suddenly, out of nowhere, a maintenance man from the summer program came by. He had a two-by-four plank in his hand as he was going to a classroom to repair a table. Seeing Riley's predicament, he walked next to Riley and said loudly, "Hey Riley, are you going to work on the fishing boat with me and the boys after school, then fish with us?"

Riley replied, "Of course."

"Just so you know," said the man, "I invited George and Evinn to meet us there."

Now, maybe George was a common name, but Evinn was not. Evinn was the county wrestling champion. Everyone knew of him. It was generally accepted that Evinn could beat anyone's butt in the school. At that point, the boys left in a hurry and were not seen in school, including in Riley's auto class, for the rest of the day.

In the classroom, Riley had learned to hold his answers to the teacher's questions and didn't care if someone else beat him to the punch. Other classmates consulted him at lunch; he often explained how to solve math problems. This brought him new friendships. One of the students he was with discussed some aggressive students in the school that were threatening him. Riley told him about his experiences at middle school as he related to Peter, who was being bullied.

Auto shop was especially fun when the instructor, John Krilling, talked about math issues on engine parts, tachometers, and car speeds, which were Riley's favorite subjects. He hoped that after a year in theory class, he would actually get to work on some of the autos.

Riley was given an assignment in one of his accelerated classes to critique any area in the district school or a local business. He chose to do his dad's elementary school.

His visit to the elementary school included visits to the classrooms, the lunchroom, the gymnasium, bathrooms, science labs, administration offices, counseling offices, outside play areas, and the grounds around the building.

The teachers who knew him from when he attended the school were happy to see him. Some even commented on how good he looked. He finished his day after talking to some of his favorite teachers and observing them in the classroom. It was a great experience for him and the teachers. Riley decided to speak to his dad and tell him what he found out during his visit.

"Well, here goes, Dad. You have kids smoking in the bathrooms. They have unhooked your detectors, so no alarms go off. The drop ceiling is not a good idea—that is where they hide cigarettes and matches until the end of the day. And they hang in the bathroom even when they don't need to use it."

"One kid was punched in the stomach in the lunchroom because he didn't give up his money to a bully. He was crying in the bathroom. One of the bullies who cornered him is a board member's son; the other is one of your friend's sons. They were using their phones to call other kids in class to spread rumors about the kid."

"Disturbingly, I saw some boys in the hallway groping a girl. And when some students entered a class late, one teacher hardly acknowledged it. The other students were being loud and disruptive in class, so maybe the teacher didn't notice the late students."

Riley bravely continued, "Teachers sit at their desks texting while students are given worksheets. I don't know how you haven't noticed this, but some teachers don't dress appropriately for class. I know sometimes on Friday or when there are special holidays you don't mind, but today was just an ordinary day. And the students don't dress appropriately either. Some girls had very short dresses, much shorter than allowed. And the guys had their pants hanging down."

"Some of the students in the classroom look older than middle school kids. I don't know if that pertains to your stay-back policy. If some of the parents of the younger kids looked carefully, they would probably say something. Especially with the short skirt issues. Having kids who are too mature with immature kids is a bad idea. I wonder if there haven't been any complaints from parents or if the teachers are not reporting the complaints."

"At the end of the day, aren't the teachers supposed to stay by their door until all the kids leave? They do not follow that. They take off as soon as the bell rings. One of the kids at the bus stop was being touched by other boys, just like I have been. The only teacher who did stick around and should have seen it seemed to look the other way. I'm guessing that reporting something like that would involve write-ups and bullying accusations."

"I have several other pages of both good and bad notes, but I wanted to point out the most obvious things to you. One more thing: It may be good to check out the boiler room every so often."

Dr. Rossey was proud of Riley and concerned about all that Riley had seen. Riley explained, "Since I lived through all these moments, it was not hard for me to make all these observations."

Anyhow, Riley got an A on the paper and said he would be more than willing to provide this to other people, but he left that up to his dad.

Throughout the year, Riley saw Mr. Alfred almost on a daily basis. And as Mr. Alfred and his men regularly waved to him or even slapped him five, Riley knew he had people looking out for him.

That's how Riley made a nice adjustment to high school. His parents and the people who knew him at the middle school could see it very clearly. Principal Toby and his assistants were super, and Riley's grades and friendships were in great shape. However, in the background, Jon Davis kept his eye on his former neighbor, with no intention of letting him have a free ride through his upcoming four years.

Despite Jon's problems in the community, he continued getting counseling, and his mother continued addressing her alcohol problem. His dad was still in prison. Jon and some of his friends seemed to always be around wherever Riley was— whether in the cafeteria, the hallway, or the gym after school, attending club activities.

As for Jon's cousin James, Mr. Davis Jr., the year was taking a downturn. A new full-time superintendent was appointed, bumping Mrs. Schossler back to the full-time principal and Mr. Davis back to the assistant principal at the middle school. This, of course, did not make Mr. Davis happy, who already had a "Principal Davis" nameplate made; he thoroughly enjoyed being in charge of more people he could tell what to do.

One day, Riley was confronted by Jon while he was getting on the school bus. "I have not forgotten what your dad did to me, so beware of what's to come. You made my mother into a worry wart and me into a criminal while my father was in prison. So you and I will be alone one day, and we will see just how much you have grown up. Believe me, you will have a real bad day when you least expect it."

Riley ignored the comments and got on the bus as Jon walked away with two other kids.

The next day, Riley was called down to the principal's office for what he thought was just a routine visit with Mr. Toby. He knew something was off when he walked in and saw Jon with Mr. Toby.

Principal Toby looked at the boys and said, "Your parents should be here momentarily, so we'll talk in a few moments." Dr. and Mrs. Rossey arrive first. Then Jon's mother, Mrs. Lisa Davis, came in accompanied by her brother-in-law, Jon's uncle, James Davis Sr., who was standing in for Jon's father, who was still in jail.

After pleasantries, Mr. Toby began the conversation by addressing Jon, "How are you doing this year in school?"

"I'm doing okay. It's a difficult adjustment after spending time in the detention center, then in an out-of-district placement," Jon said strategically, giving a nasty look to Dr. Rossey.

Mr. Toby continued, "Jon, have you had any problems at the bus zone at the end of the school day?"

"No, not really."

"How about you, Riley?"

"No, not really."

"Have you two seen each other at the loading zone?"

"A couple of times."

"Have there been any problems?"

"No, not really," both boys again respond.

"Jon, do you know what it means to threaten another student?"

"Yes, of course."

"But you have not threatened anyone here, have you?"

At that point, Mrs. Davis became defensive. "Okay, what is going on?"

"Allow me to play a recording for you."

As Mr. Toby plays the recording, Mrs. Davis says, "Okay. Stop it." She looked at Jon and said, "May I have a word alone with my son?"

"By all means," said Mr. Toby as he directed them to his conference room and closed the door. The next thing you know, everyone heard a ruckus as Mrs. Davis slammed Jon's head into the table. Bursting open the door and seeing the blood coming from Jon's head, Mr. Davis Sr. and Dr. Rossey grabbed Jon's mom and attempted to hold her back from going after him again. Within two minutes, the school police entered the room, grabbed Mrs. Davis, handcuffed her, and took her away. The school nurse quickly arrived to treat Jon.

Mr. Davis, his face flushed red, furiously verbally confronted Mr. Toby, "That sneak attack was completely unnecessary. That child could be seriously hurt," and now including Dr. Rossey, continued, "and you principals are to blame. We are going to sue the school."

"Go right ahead," Mr. Toby calmly replied. "This tape recording came from an anonymous person who saw Jon harassing Riley. He recorded the conversation and turned it over to me."

Mr. Alfred, who just happened to be nearby and heard the commotion, had let himself into the principal's office. "That's amazing that one of the students would actually tell on Jon."

"Well, that's not actually true. You see, our maintenance man, Lou, had the tape recorder on and did not see any reason to interrupt as Riley handled things well. But he did turn on his walkie-talkie, and, as I sat in my office, I heard the conversation."

Jon had to go to the hospital. He was bandaged up and released into the care of his Uncle James, the senior Mr. Davis. Jon's mom was booked for assault at police headquarters and held in jail pending an appearance before the judge. Jon was placed on a home instruction program under the supervision of Mr. Davis Sr., pending a report to the School Board and a meeting to take place.

With the incident behind him, Riley continued on with his new normal. Other than a few minor incidents, Riley enjoyed the year hanging out with Betzy and making new friends.

At the end of the school year, Betzy and Riley were announced as the two top academic students in their class. Betzy's brothers continued to keep a protective eye on her, but they kept their distance. They began to see a different Riley Rossey than they had heard about at middle school.

Chapter 19

Sophomore Year

After freshman year, Riley had another very successful summer. Besides hanging out with Mr. Alfred hunting and fishing, he occasionally got together with Betzy and made daily trips to the gym, meeting with a trainer his parents provided. Riley also became more involved in church activities and became good friends with several people he met in auto shop and computer repair. He discovered he loved helping his neighbors and friends. In fact, he had success in helping a friend get an old auto up and running.

Riley's grandfather had been very much drawn to old vehicles himself, and Riley's dad decided it was time to show Riley a garage he had been renting to tinker with cars. He was hoping to get Riley involved with some projects. When Riley first entered the garage, he almost fainted at the site of the autos.

"Grandpa willed these autos to you?" Riley was so excited and began spending hours upon hours examining and learning about the cars.

Working out daily to keep his body in shape became a must, not a maybe. Keeping up with the latest dress was equally important. Compared to his middle school self, Riley continued to grow more and more unrecognizable. He looked athletic, dressed great, and his hairstyle was always current. But most importantly of all, his attitude had adjusted as he learned to listen, think, and respond appropriately to people.

He had quality time to spend with Betzy to learn more about her. "You know that I come from a broken home. My father left me and my two brothers when I was five, and I have pretty much been protected by my two brothers since then. Cheerleading was always my relief from stress, particularly when my mom was crying or feeling so guilty. I learned how to take care of myself, study hard, and be a friend, not worrying about those who were not really my friends. The guys that are popular are not half as smart as you. They dress great and have nice cars, but they are pretty dumb. They are turned off by me because I get good grades and am, like you, hungry for knowledge."

Riley responded, "Well, you certainly have that cheerleader look: blonde hair, blue eyes, and you are very pretty."

Betzy and Riley hung out together—not dating, not holding hands, just friends. Some of the kids found it hard to believe. "Hey, Tommy, it looks like your sister is going steady with that Rossey kid," said one of his friends.

Betzy's brother said, "I have talked to my sister, and that is not the case. Stop spreading rumors."

After the incident with his mom, Jon Davis was temporarily placed in a foster home out of the district. Of course, the Davis clan still blamed the Rosseys and vowed to get even. Mrs. Davis was placed under house arrest and in a mandatory alcohol anonymous program.

Riley continued his transformation even though James Davis at the middle school was still in the district and hung on tightly to memories of Riley. Mr. Alfred and Riley continued to see each other almost every day somewhere in the school.

During lunch one day, Principal Toby came over and sat with Riley in the lunchroom just to talk. "Some of my friends in auto shop have to work to help their families. They can't even come to school because of it. Can we get them in night school?" Riley asked thoughtfully. Feeling brave, he added, "Sometimes, other students think the vocational kids are dumb and don't have a place around the bright kids. I resent that."

Mr. Toby listened carefully and said, "You know what? I proposed having dually certified teachers teaching at night so every student can get a regular diploma, even when they have to work while getting high school credit. It always amazes me that we cater to students like you who are academically brighter but disregard flexibility for other students."

Riley's size and build made some students wonder whether he would ever play team sports. But it was clear that was not where Riley's future lay, so it was a short-lived thought. Riley was an academic wizard; everyone knew a solid financial future was his if he wanted it. But there were roads ahead necessary for him to take to get there.

One day, Riley was sitting with Mr. Alfred and his crew in the morning and asked thoughtfully, "Why can't we have adults attend school during the daytime? It seems that adults who work night shifts never quite get that opportunity. Many of the maintenance and custodial crew could actually benefit; Mr. Toby is certainly open to the idea."

Riley continued to contemplate this idea, and as he brought it up more, serious discussions ensued. A survey was even created to gauge interest, which the Board heard about. They were intrigued for several reasons. Having adults at school during the day could be a model that would help many motivated community members who never had the opportunity to finish high school. It would also add more mature members to the high school classes. However, opponents did not want young girls to be exposed to adults that early in their lives.

Riley's dad said, "Riley, you have so many open discussions about what can make schools better. Why don't you enter the field of education?"

"Dad, I can't wait to get out of school. Why would I want to stay there? Also, there is no real incentive to make a lot of money in the educational system, like in other financial industries."

During his sophomore year, Riley continued on the road to social recovery. However, there were still several students from elementary and middle school who were loyal to Jon. Also, James Davis still had a vendetta with the Rosseys.

Riley's interest in computers and autos grew even more as he fit the electives into his very tight schedule. His dad got various vehicles donated to the school so the students could learn more about cars, including new designs, options, and the operation of the new computers in cars. The auto teacher was amazed at Riley's troubleshooting ability and gave Riley more and more complex problems to solve. As far as computers were concerned, Riley also showed an ability to repair them.

All in all, Riley made great progress during his sophomore year. Betzy and he were ranked first and second in their class, which surprised no one. His grades, social recovery, and knowledge were now far beyond that of any high school.

Chapter 20

Junior Year

Junior year was a critical time as Riley would take standardized tests, college boards, and apply to colleges. During the summer, he spent much of his time studying about colleges and learning other important information to determine where he would be headed after high school. His desire was to major in finance.

Two of his friends at school, Hakeem and Marshall, both wanted to continue learning how to repair computers. They even thought about drumming up business outside of school. When Mr. Alfred and the supervisor of the computers at the school, Mark Donnelly, said there were many outdated computers stored away, Riley suggested that he and his friends could practice fixing and cleaning them. Then maybe they could even be used in the lower grades in the district.

After several months, this resourceful team made several hundred computers work like new again. Principal Toby was so impressed that he informed the Board of Education, who was also thoroughly impressed with Riley, Hakeem, and Marshall.

Then, as part of their education, the boys were sent to other schools in the district to service their computers. Mr. Davis, who never forgot a Rossey, made it impossible for Riley to get his hands on the computers at the middle school. Every day, there was another excuse why the students could not come to the school to repair the computers. Additionally, Mr. Davis began to spread a rumor that the boys were making money from this computer operation.

In response, Mr. Alfred began having his crew take their time attending to Mr. Davis's emergency repairs. Mr. Davis finally got the message, and suddenly, the middle school had an open door for Riley and his computer repair crew. And there were no more complaints or accusations.

As the school year progressed, Betzy and Riley became closer friends. They again had all their top honors classes together and continued to rank first and second academically.

Riley asked his father to give him more information about his grandfather, who had passed away shortly after he retired. And his father shared some enlightening stories.

"Grandpa was a very bright individual who seemed to make things happen that you never expected. For example, when there were worries about vandalism in the school at night, Grandpa set a trap and nailed the offenders right away."

"Then there was the time he was walking home from school when two boys were about to jump him. Out of nowhere, a large tree branch fell and hit the two boys, knocking them out."

"Another time, at a high school baseball game, Grandpa was sitting in the bleachers when a home run was hit. The guy in front of him should have caught the ball, but it bounced and landed in Grandpa's large soda cup."

"Even stranger, one day, as he was driving in a snowstorm, cars were skidding all around him. Every car in the area was hit except his."

"But the king of all the strange things happened when he was the high school principal. He went into the media center as the lights went out in the school. Rather than scrambling and getting all the students excited, he snapped his fingers, according to several witnesses, and suddenly, the lights and power came back on. This wasn't anybody's imagination—three students saw it with their own eyes. After that day, students in the high school were scared to death of your grandpa."

"He retired very early in life and then, out of nowhere, became very sick and died. He left behind many significant sayings. One very popular one was, 'What goes around comes around and winds up biting people in the back when they least expected it.' He always said that a voice in his ear kept telling him, 'Your place in life is in the school system.' And when he followed that voice, his life changed. Guess who one of his best friends was? None other than Andrew Alfred, father of your friend, Archie Alfred."

Riley enjoyed attending some of the school's sporting events, particularly the football games, where Betzy was one of the cheerleaders. Riley was now well respected and looked upon as a good friend by many of his fellow students.

Riley's parents also grew in their ways, learning from how Riley handled things. Although Dr. Rossey got angry at Mr. Davis for not allowing Riley to fix the old computers at the middle school, he came to feel sorry for him, recognizing he had so many family problems.

While Riley was in his auto shop class, he decided to ask the maintenance and custodial staff if they wanted or needed oil changes. They all agreed and came at different times for Riley and his friends to complete the oil changes. It was a small way to pay them back for all they had done for him.

Riley became known as "Rebuilt Riley." Everything about him had changed. When he spoke with some of his middle school teachers at church, he said one sentence changed his life, "Desire to change." He desired to change himself and the world, and he became determined that nothing would stop him. Riley continued to use his gift of problem-solving to help other students with math and even worked with his teacher on very complex, college-level problems.

In just a couple of years, Riley had gone from being a victim of bullies to being known as the kid who went the extra mile to help others, even those who had mistreated him. When he thought about his past, he concluded, "I guess being bullied and ridiculed was just what I needed to straighten out my life." And then he considered, "How can I help other bullied kids get their freedom from bullies and change their lives forever? I've learned to have fun in school, and I love my classes and my friends. I want every student to feel that way."

Riley even took some night classes in auto shop and computer repair. The next part of his academic life was about to begin as he searched for the right college to attend. His biggest struggle in that area was that almost every college he applied to accepted him.

Phil DeFranco, the high school's math supervisor, and Riley developed a close relationship. Mr. Defranco was awed at how bright Riley was at solving math problems and how good he was at teaching others. Several students who asked

Riley for help with their math at lunch began to problem-solve with a different voice. All Mr. DeFranco could say was "Wow" when students who had previously struggled began to hand in excellent work after getting Riley's help.

One day after school, several cheerleaders, including Betzy, were headed to the parking to go home after practice. Betzy's friend, Michelle, seemed to be having car trouble. Riley happened to be near and asked if he could help. Meanwhile, all the cheerleaders were calling their boyfriends and parents for rides.

Within minutes, Riley started the car, saying, "Bring the car to the shop tomorrow. I'll make a couple more adjustments so you don't have that problem again."

Michelle's boyfriend, Hurley Johnson, one of the several football players who was never really nice to Riley, was surprised when he heard about what happened. The next day in the cafeteria, Hurley walked up to Riley and thanked him for helping Michelle, saying, "I'll pay you for any parts."

Riley said, "No worries. We have filters and other parts donated to the school. And there is a minimal service charge."

Hurley replied, "Listen, if you would like to come to our party after Friday's game at George Trent's house and greet our players, you would be welcome."

Riley accepted.

When Riley and his friends attended the party, Betzy's brothers walked up to him and thanked him for always being nice to Betzy. Then Michelle's boyfriend made a toast to Riley, and the kids all joined in. Riley thanked the group and, at the end of the night, left feeling really good about himself. Riley even announced that he would always be available to check out any personal computers or vehicles anyone had problems with.

Riley's parents were very happy to hear all the good news, but Mr. Alfred made the best comment. "Mr. Davis has no idea about the quality person and the character he has helped to come out of hiding from the boiler room. We are scheduling a fishing trip after church this Sunday. You and your dad are coming with my crew and our summer team."

At that point, it seemed like high school would have a happy ending for Riley. As we've seen, however, life can take drastic turns, and for Riley, his high school career would not have a fairy tale ending.

Chapter 21

Senior Year

Riley was accepted at all the top-name colleges, but staying close to home was a priority for him. Meanwhile, sadly for Riley, Betzy decided to attend a specific college for medical specialists across the country, on the West Coast. But they still had a full year ahead of them.

As senior year progressed, Riley continued to do well, proving he was well-rounded in all aspects of life. Unfortunately, his old bullies raised their ugly heads. Plasner and his groupies and the Davis clan came roaring back for another round. Mr. Alfred continually reminded the students who actually ran this place and this town.

It all began at the senior outing. Before the bike race, John Plasner and his friends decided to ensure Riley's bike tires would go flat during the race. Mr. Alfred, keenly aware of what they were doing, switched Riley's and John's tires. As a result, Plasner's bike became the one with the slight leek.

Much to John Plasner's surprise, his bike collapsed during the race while Riley finished in the top three. However, Mr. Alfred didn't think that was enough of a payback.

During the dodgeball game, one of Mr. Alfred's boys loaded up a special ball and made sure it ended up in Riley's hands. Riley threw the ball directly at John's groin, and bingo, a bull's eye where the sun doesn't shine. The pain was obvious as down went John for the ten-count. He was taken away in a wheelchair, barfing up a storm. It just seemed like Riley could do no wrong.

All the senior activities were equally rewarding. But the three main events of the year, the senior trip, the school prom, and graduation night, were still to come.

The prom was the next senior event. John and his buddies hoped they could get at least one more good shot at Riley. They planned to plant a bottle of whiskey in Riley's car before the event, hoping Riley would get caught. But just in case, they then planned to put a bag of weed at the table where he would be sitting. That would be followed by having the trunk of Riley's car loaded with beer at the end of the night. (They would pull this off thanks to one of John's friends who would take Riley's car keys from the valet parking attendant.)

This time, they knew the triple whammy would succeed. No one would see it coming. What they didn't know, however, was that Riley's summertime friends were more keenly aware and devised a plan to beat John and his gang at their own game. You see, it just so happened that one of the valets was friends with Evinn, a friend of Riley's, and learned of the setup.

With the prom underway, as Betzy and Riley were having dinner, things began to unfold.

As administrators within the district, both Mr. Davis and Dr. Rossey were invited to attend the senior events. However, Dr. and Mrs. Rossey decided to let this be Riley's night and declined the invitation. Mr. Davis, aware that there would be some sort of revenge, also planned to stay clear of the prom so his own name would not be associated with any happenings.

While the early entertainment and dinner were going on, some girls who were jealous of Betzy and were accomplices in the plan warned the administrators that several girls, including Betzy, were with guys who brought liquor and weed to the prom.

After being spoken to and questioned, Riley agreed to let the security teachers search his car. Nothing showed up, baffling Plasner and his boys. Frustrated, John and Jon (Plasner and Davis) banded together to pick a fight with Riley while in line for the picture booth.

But it was Riley who pulled off the surprise of the night. He got out his cell phone, which showed all the pre-prom activities of the boys, including taking Riley's keys from the valet. Jon was in shock, and he was quickly brought to the attention of the administrators and even more quickly escorted out of the prom.

"How did this happen?" asked John Plasner. The boys' dates were beyond angry as they fled before any more strange stuff began to happen.

Meanwhile, in the background, Mr. Alfred and Evinn appeared smiling. Riley smiled at them and gave them a thumbs-up signal.

The next school day, Principal Toby called in the Davis clan. Mr. Davis was finally smart enough not to show his face. Jon was again placed on homebound instruction and banned from all further graduation activities, including graduation itself. The Davis clan was temporarily disbanded.

But one more strange event, which smelled like a Davis job, took place. It seemed that the mathematical computation of the grade point averages, determining the valedictorian and the salutatorian, were somehow messed with. Betzy was advised by one of the teachers that the results were so close that Dr. Rossey insisted Riley be named the top student as he had progressed so far. That infuriated Betzy, bringing her to tears. "It can't be true. Dr. Rossey was never like that. But I guess maybe I just didn't see him for what he was."

When Riley found out, he confronted his dad.

"What are you talking about?" Dr. Rossey asked. "I was not even part of the committee, so how could I weigh in?" So the mystery continued.

With the graduation activities over and Riley not attending many of the graduation parties as he and Betzy were not speaking, high school ended on a sad note.

Chapter 22

After High School Graduation

During the summer, Riley was constantly told he was now entering the real world—there was no more high school with all its little problems. The time had come to put up or shut up.

Riley spent his summer fishing with Mr. Alfred, who enjoyed learning even more about him. Riley knew he had a lifetime friend. Everyone was surprised when he decided not to stay in the area but to go to a mid-western school. He hoped this would be far enough away to forget Betzy and the Davis family. The end of the school year had been so totally frustrating.

Riley believed he had his career all set. He had the smarts, had researched all the courses, and was ready for a new challenge. This would be his first time away from home, and he knew there would be challenges ahead, including getting used to different weather.

Riley also would have a roommate at Great West University, someone he knew little about. He didn't know what to expect but intended to be an excellent roommate himself.

When he arrived on campus, Riley looked like any college freshman and knew he would be happy to be able to communicate well with his fellow students and the staff. Since Betzy and Riley were no longer a pair, he would not have that distraction to worry about. They had spoken after the graduation fiasco but had decided to break ties to keep themselves on task. They both knew that if they did happen to see each other, it would be a very short reunion. Riley's parents and Betzy's mom were very supportive of their decision.

It was time to meet Juan Brown, Riley's roommate. Juan was an inner-city kid from New York, originally from Puerto Rico. It did not take long for the two of them to hit it off. Juan was a good-looking kid who was at school on an athletic scholarship. They spent time learning about each other from the start.

One night, Juan and Riley decided to go to the local hangout, have a drink, and get to know each other better. As they walked in, three men approached them, one of whom called out to Juan using derogatory terms. This was disturbing, but the boys walked away and treated it as an isolated incident.

Their response, however, was not taken well by the three young men. Riley said to them, "We are not looking for trouble."

"Why don't we go elsewhere?" Juan suggested.

But as they made their way to the door, the three men followed them. Again, Riley said, "We are just going to go. You three gentlemen have a great evening."

One of the three decided to block the doorway, and before Riley could say another word, an unknown, aggressive guy violently pushed the guy blocking the door aside. When the other friends went to assist him, they were both knocked down by this stranger. Thinking that the person was a friend of Juan and Riley's, the three men left the bar nursing their wounds.

Riley and Juan walked over to thank the stranger, who turned out to be an ex-Navy Seal who saw what was happening and did not like it. "Thank you," said the boys.

The man introduced himself as Derf. "Listen," he said, "You call me at this number if you ever have any problems. I assure you, you have special protection from me. By the way, my friend, a fisherman from the north, told me to say hello to you."

The boys were not really sure how to take this, but Riley had an idea who the fisherman was.

Juan and Riley began to hang out together all the time. They discovered through their talks that they both were bullied at an early age. Riley found that pretty amazing given Juan's size and build. "I used my workouts and my passion for workouts to get this far."

"So, opposites really do attract. I used my brains to get by," laughed Riley. Their support for each other continued as the weekends passed by and their friendship grew.

With the Thanksgiving and Christmas holidays coming up quickly, Juan and Riley planned to visit each other's families together, which made both sets of parents very happy.

Juan came to school as a member of the football team, but he quickly decided that would be short-lived. He had always thought about being a physical education teacher and coach and decided to pursue that track.

After hearing about Juan's career goals, Riley woke up one morning after a dream about his grandpa and said, "Oh my gosh, that is where I should be headed as well." He didn't know for sure how this came to him, but how Juan explained it resonated with him like a voice from above.

Juan explained, "My life growing up sucked in many ways. I know I can teach kids how to deal with being picked on better than anyone."

"WOW," said Riley. "I can't believe you said that."

Juan continued, "I can kick butt in the class, make the kids love school, and make the bullies feel like their days are numbered. Look at us! We met each other, and we're having fun. We volunteer for groups we belong to. And we are both staying away from fraternities because hazing is not our thing. And we are doing pretty good. Excellent, even."

One night while attending a party, Riley and Juan met some of the athletes and some of the brightest students. During the conversation, a young lady asked Riley if he happened to know anyone who fixed computers. It did not take long for word to spread about Riley and his computer skills.

Then, just as it happened in the past, one day when Juan and Riley were leaving their dormitory, a fellow student's car wouldn't start, so Riley helped her. Another young lady saw what was going on and, intrigued, came over and introduced herself.

Charise Montez was very attractive and friendly. Riley later found out she was a cheerleader. The two friends, after finishing with the car, invited Charise to go to the local coffee house with them. There, she showed them a picture of herself as a freshman in high school, which floored Riley and Juan. Charise—overweight, with pimples, and not looking happy—did not look like the same girl. The Charise in front of them was attractive, smiling, and confident. They also found out she was a native of Trinidad. Riley was excited to learn everything about her.

"You know, Riley, my parents made such a stink about me being on the cheerleading squad. Everyone knew how they pushed me. It was embarrassing. I said to the coach, 'If I'm not making it, please cut me.' When I said that, the coach responded, 'You will not only make it, but you will be a star.'"

That someone could offer her that kind of encouragement blew Riley away.

Riley was inspired by Charise's attitude and couldn't wait to follow some of her advice. He knew he still had much room to grow. He worked to implement improvements in who he was each day. Sure enough, he matured as he intentionally chose the habits and attitude he wanted to be evident in his life.

"Who I will be is up to me. Not my parents. Not a counselor, my teacher, or even my friends. It is 100% my choice."

Chapter 23

CHANGE OF MAJORS

Charise and Riley began hanging out regularly and became good friends. Charise was majoring in education and was planning on becoming an elementary teacher.

"Listen, I'd like you to talk to my dad, who is an elementary school principal. He could give you great insight into what makes a great teacher."

As he talked with Charise, Riley kept getting the urge to take the plunge himself and change majors. He went back and forth—first, it was yes, then it was no. But finally, the yes won.

Riley could have talked all day about how horrible school had been for him. His memories of middle school were the worst, thanks to Mr. Davis. But because of that, he knew he could have a positive effect on many students who feel like they have no choice but to suffer through school.

With his decision made, Riley called his mom and dad. "Why all of a sudden?" asked his mom and dad.

"Well, I've met two people who have had a very good effect on me. They've also reminded me of who my mom, dad, grandpa, and grandma are."

Riley would study secondary education with a major in English and math. The big question was, would he stick to it? Or would he be reminded about his bad experiences in the early grades and back out?

After meeting with and surprising his college counselor, he walked away smiling with a plan to accelerate his coursework. His grades and the teachers all agreed that Riley was more than capable of making this work.

The redirection required Riley to take an enormous number of courses during intersession and summer. He had online courses and plans for future courses.

Nobody ever moved as fast through this number of classes. The best part was that Riley aced them all.

Riley and Charise stayed close during the summer. One night, he even snuck into her dormitory and ended up spending the night with her studying, talking, and laughing. That was a huge step for this kid who was supposed to be scared and shaky. He could not believe that he actually felt that comfortable with a female. The two were so close that Charise began attending church with Riley.

One night back in Mason, Dr. Rossey got a phone call from Betzy Lajourner's mom just to say hello. As they were talking, Betzy's mom told Dr. Rossey something she had learned about the controversial class rankings from the year before. Mr. Davis had been dating the senior class advisor, and they had sabotaged the whole thing. What she couldn't figure out was why Davis let Riley win top student.

"Easy," said Riley's dad. "He screwed up."

The parents ended their conversation, vowing to keep in contact. Secretly, they both hoped that one day Betzy and Riley would get back together.

Riley often thought about how exciting it would be to return to his old neighborhood as a teacher. "Call it what you want, but I think it would be great to get back to my old school district and create what I feel has been my destiny. Nothing would make me feel as good as helping students who hate school learn to love it."

As he considered this as his future, Riley often thought about Mr. Alfred, hoping he would still be working at the district when Riley returned on his new mission. He also considered Mr. Davis and the ongoing destructive role he played. "I certainly would not mind catching Mr. Davis in a noncompromising position, so the school system would be forced to take a close look at that man."

Chapter 24

Student Teaching

Riley completed most of his academic courses and was finally prepared to begin student teaching. He was placed in the inner city—with his background in rural Pennsylvania and Iowa, this was a totally new experience for him. Juan helped him understand how kids from poorer areas function. Riley learned that despite many similarities to his own experiences, he would likely need more patience and a different kind of understanding. "Believe me, there are bullies from all walks of life and all ages," said Juan. Riley certainly could attest to that.

The first time out with his cooperating teacher in his shadow, Riley was immediately thrown into the deep end. After being introduced to the class, he was tasked with presenting his first lesson. Unfortunately, the teacher with whom he was working was not the strongest disciplinarian, which left both teaching and discipline to Riley.

"Hey, what are you trying to teach us?" said one of the students, which unnerved Riley a bit.

One advantage became clear, however. Riley had learned conversational Spanish in school and so was able to communicate with some of the Hispanic students. This was a comfort for them.

After his first day, a feeling-out process for the teacher and students, Juan and Riley decided to sit down and write out some strategies for this unruly bunch of kids. Charise and Nicki chimed in. "You have worked too hard to get to this point. You cannot let a few minor inconveniences stop you from getting where you want to go. Use the strengths you have and make the necessary adjustments."

Since most of the students in the class liked basketball, football, and music, Riley improvised. He made sure the material was appropriately presented, working his lessons around sports and statistics to get the students excited. It worked! Riley brought in music lyrics, basketball and football stats, and even purchased sports magazines.

When presented with questions he didn't have the answer to, Riley unashamedly located the answers on his class computer with ease. He also gave students permission to look up information on their cell phones. But if Riley beat them to the answers, he would hold their phones until the end of the period.

In class, they discussed life-relevant topics such as paychecks, salaries, deductions, and savings—all without the students even realizing it. Students began reaching into their pockets for money as Riley taught them how to multiply even the smallest amount. Not surprisingly, several of the students had wads of bills in their pockets. Juan explained that's life in the inner city.

The students could not believe how Riley brought information to the class in easy-to-understand language. They wanted to know more. They learned how players in the sports and entertainment industry got started and how important it was to learn continually and incorporate new methods into everything they do.

The supervising teacher and the college supervisor were thrilled. "Riley is a natural. He is able to motivate the students."

"For example," the teacher said, "Joansy would just sit in my class and not even open up her book or look at me. To see how she's working with other students now is amazing."

Riley would stay up all night and concentrate on innovative ways to address their learning. He made students feel important; teaching them to become leaders was his real specialty.

This formerly scared, bullied kid was now making some of the most difficult, hard-core students become learners. The disruption everyone expected to come with a new student teacher never materialized.

With Riley's computer skills, he also showed students ways to make the computer work for them. He would take the students to the computer lab, where the classroom teacher always feared that students would get kicked out of the class. The school administrators entering the classroom could not believe these were the same kids who had caused disruptions. Riley created interesting learning experiences in the lab. Even some of the veteran teachers in the school watched in awe as Riley stood in front of the class like a motivational speaker. He had the kids screaming out answers to his questions.

Jaxson, a student who had been suspended several times and made a great turnaround, was later asked what the difference was between Mr. Rossey and other teachers he disrespected. "The difference is Mr. Rossey was a real man. He didn't stand in front of the class and try to con us. He got my respect right away, and I knew I was going to learn something. He has been part of my success."

Riley's second practice teaching assignment seemed to be right up his avenue—he would teach a class to some of the highest-level students in an upper-middle-class district.

Not knowing what to expect, Riley entered the class and noticed several students texting on their phones and others talking to each other. The teacher started to scream, threatening to give extra assignments and to recommend to the students' coaches and advisors that they not be allowed to participate in extra-curricular activities. Riley knew those threats would only lead to more negative behavior.

One student sitting in the back of the class caught Riley's eye. He looked similar to what Riley looked like when he was in school. He wore thick glasses, was very overweight, and had a headset on to block out everything around him. The worst part was that neither the teacher nor the other students paid any attention to him at all.

When Riley questioned the classroom teacher about that student, he said, "Michael is in his own world. He doesn't talk to anyone, doesn't interrupt class, and has no friends here or, really, anywhere in the school."

"Don't his parents get upset?"

"His parents are happy he is not home disturbing them."

Although Riley clearly recognized a picture of himself, he was surprised that none of the kids seemed to be picking on him.

So Riley began teaching with Michael on his mind. *How do I get to him?*

Riley decided to read Michael's file to learn more about him. Riley's dad always warned against making assumptions about someone without taking the time to learn how they tick.

Michael had been a foster child and was adopted by his present parents when he was five years old. He always felt that his parents prioritized their two biological children. Their daughters were honor students, and, reading between the lines, Riley discovered that the parents had long ago accepted that Michael would never measure up to his sisters. Michael's birth parents had a checkered past, and it seemingly never dawned on his adoptive parents that their son could be very intelligent. Riley reasoned that this unfortunate scenario only added to Michael's many emotional scars, which surely inhibited his maturity.

So Riley began to challenge Michael in math with very difficult problems, which Michael seemed to love. Instead of calling on him, Riley provided special worksheets covering the same lesson he presented to the rest of the class. He discovered that Michael had some special talents that were never tapped.

Then there was Jeffrey, another one of those kids who looked and acted very smart. The more questions Riley asked him, the more a really bright and innovative child emerged.

Riley also made inroads with several other students. He offered to meet them after school for tutoring. As they came to trust him, many students opened up to him about their present everyday life. He would ask them questions such as—Why are you absent so much? Why are you often late for school? What does your home life look like? Do you have a space to study?

Additionally, to his fellow staff, Riley would ask—How do you find out what is going on with kids other in the school? What about the staff in the school who are not in the classrooms—what part do they play? What are the politics of the school, and how does it affect teachers in the classroom? Why are some students allowed to do certain things in the classroom and others are not?

Riley's cooperating teacher could not believe how well the students worked with him. Riley brought many of them out of their shells. He saw himself in the students and began to see a pattern of how he reacted when he was their age.

One morning, Riley began class by describing the problems he had when he was in their shoes. "I would like to change the subject this morning to talk about who I am, how I handled school peer pressure, and how I screwed up. I often knew the answers and would shout them out even before the teacher finished the question. Boy, did that make the other kids mad. What I later learned was that it actually made them feel stupid and insecure. They thought I was trying to be the teacher's pet by kissing up. That got my butt kicked."

"I dressed differently than other kids, too. And I don't just mean because I didn't wear hot-name clothes. I didn't do the basics, which included wearing pressed clothes, wearing my correct size, or even clothes from my generation."

All this transparency brought laughter, but it also brought a better understanding of their own circumstances. The students took great interest in Riley's stories and listened intensely.

"I never attempted to make friends with the opposite sex, although I was friendly with one female because we were both studious and challenged each other—that sometimes breaks the ice. It is important to have friends who will stand by you. For the most part, I was unaware of this social dynamic. Because I did things above my age level, I was never part of the in-crowd."

"But my biggest problem was that I was targeted consistently by one bully who did not want me to have any freedom. It became a family feud thing, and it continued until the last day of high school."

Before he could finish, hands flew up, including Michael's and Jeffrey's. The questions were not part of the curriculum, but that class turned into a real question-and-answer, student-to-teacher and teacher-to-student experience.

Riley also utilized other techniques he had learned the hard way. His dad used to say that every kid is different, even if they come from the same family or the same neighborhood. Riley would share with anyone who would listen, "As a teacher, it is my job to see what makes each kid in the classroom tick. How do you do that with so many levels of kids from different families and some growing up in different parts of the country? My father always said, 'That is why you are blessed as a teacher. It is something that you are either blessed with or not. It comes from very deep within.' But my biggest blessing is having the opportunity to connect with students—and I can only do that because of what I have gone through."

Chapter 25

Accelerating His Coursework

As Riley seriously dove into the change of direction for his career, loading his coursework at a feverish pace, he and Juan banded together on their coursework. Although recreation and the idea of being a college student were exciting, Juan and Riley were far more concerned about their teaching career and how far they could go.

Riley often thought about Betzy and how badly his relationship with her ended. Not only had Betzy's mom come forward with more information from the ranking scandal, but his dad learned more negative information.

Juan and Riley decided to set up a business similar to what Riley had done during high school. They taught computer secrets and did math tutoring, as Juan had nearly the same skill set in computers as Riley. This made it easy for the two to combine their knowledge and set up a service.

Not only did they find students knocking down their door to learn about computers, but students also requested to be taught various skills to help them organize their college life. Some students asked for help with classwork besides math, which expanded their tutoring business. Riley would not accept any money for his services if the student could not afford it. Many professors were not very happy with this offer as they had their own private tutoring services and were earning quite a nice piece of change on the side.

One day, while he was tutoring an international student in the library, one of the professors came in and asked Riley why he thought he was a better tutor. Riley responded. "Listen, Professor Jastot, I am not trying to steal your thunder. I just know my stuff and want to help students."

After that, Professor Jastot returned every paper Riley turned in covered with unsubstantiated issues marked in red. Riley confronted the professor, but his B-grades continued. Riley wondered how this was supposed to be a good learning model. He knew he never turned in anything worth less than an A.

Chapter 26

GRADUATING AND GETTING HIS FIRST JOB

Doubling up on coursework, Riley finished up all his required courses and was ready to graduate early. His parents encouraged him to seek a job as a substitute near his home district. The downside was that returning home would break up Riley's daily relationship with Charise. Juan planned to return to Puerto Rico, but they would still communicate and hoped to see each other during the holidays and summer.

Riley received all the necessary certifications quickly and was soon ready to teach. His mom encouraged the administrators to seek out Riley for an interview; they discovered that Riley was everything his mom claimed. Riley was appointed as a permanent substitute teacher, especially for all the honors and accelerated classes. With his strong background in science, history, English, and math and a proven track record for resiliency, it was his big chance to head home and show people what Riley Rossey was all about. So, in victory, Riley returned home, making his family very happy.

Dr. Rossey always said kids recognize a phony educator better than anyone. He knew his son was no phony and expected Riley to work effectively with all the teachers and students. Soon, students, teachers, and administrators began to realize that Riley was a special talent. He brought a great attitude to work, and the students loved his approach. It wasn't long before all the kids hoped they would have Mr. Rossey teach their class. Parents, hearing about his story and his special ability to get through to students, liked that their children were in Riley's classes, even as a substitute.

Mr. Rossey's teaching was enhanced by his desire to get to work early and stay late so he could offer students extra help. He also provided his students with his email, which also helped the parents, who no longer felt alone trying to figure out the newest parts of the curriculum. Mr. Rossey often ate lunch with kids in the cafeteria and was available to them during his preparation periods.

In class, students always wanted to know more about how Mr. Rossey had turned his life around. He was a great teacher and an even better role model. A few teachers resented the time he put in, but Riley handled that very diplomatically.

When it came time to schedule the staff for the following year, a math teacher Riley had substituted for many times told the administration she would not be returning. This was perfect for Riley to hear, though he never imagined being in this position as a student. Riley never forgot what it meant to be bullied and dread attending school. At one time, expecting Riley to work in a school district was as far-fetched as thinking he would become President of the United States. Zero possibility. But as his mom used to say, "Never say never."

So he became a full-fledged teacher, but that did not stop his desire to learn. During the next year, Riley took extra courses, working towards his master's degree in math. "I know this will not be the end of my education," Riley declares. "I am headed for a doctorate, like my father and grandfather. And I will think about an administrative position in the future."

Riley had certainly proven he was everything the district had been looking for. He owed his teaching style directly to what his mom, dad, and grandparents had taught him over the years.

With his father's influence, Riley imagined his future as a school administrator. "If I start interviewing now, I can get a head start with the experience that I will need to succeed." As he spoke to other administrators, he picked up many little helpful pointers. His dad contacted some of his administrative friends to have mock interviews with Riley. "He has the Rossey pedigree," they relayed to his dad.

Despite his aspirations, Riley knew he wanted to continue influencing students as a teacher. "I know one thing for sure. I will always want to teach at least one class a day regardless of the position I am appointed to."

Riley continued to work hard and be creative in his teaching, bringing other teachers and administrators in on the lessons. He was very confident in his future and intentionally kept learning from other teachers and through his attendance in college courses. "Dad always said that he learns more from the students than they learn from him. That's a pretty serious comment."

Riley worked feverishly to finish his master's degree and become eligible for his doctorate. He had all the tools. His co-workers agreed, one of them saying, "He knows kids and has a great rapport with the kids and the parents."

Riley humbly stated, "The educational world changes so quickly that we have to improve on a daily basis. The days of being a generalist and not a specialist are gone. Research not only makes better teachers but brings information to students as well. I'm a lifelong learner, and I hope my students take the same road."

Riley's classes were always full—he told students and their parents that a missed day of school is information lost that would help their learning. Riley's mom and dad knew great things were ahead for their son.

Chapter 27

Mr. Rossey Stands Out

Mr. Rossey's teaching schedule began to include both lower and higher-level math classes. This pleased him as his goal was to reach students at all levels. "It's strange to me that high school administrators in this school system always think it's better to look at the top classes. Not the case for me. You learn more from the bottom than from the top."

The administration got wind of the fact that Riley always ate lunch in the cafeteria with the students and also maintained a "breakfast club." So they said, what the heck, and assigned him café duty, which, although unfair, did not bother Riley.

Riley applied for many of the after-school and weekend club activities. That was okay with the other teachers. Most of them would not apply for the jobs because they were too low paying for too many hours.

One day, the teachers decided to have a slowdown—to just abide by their contracts and nothing else. Meanwhile, Riley became very creative in the classroom. Many of the staff were dazzled by his teaching methods and how he was getting the attention of some of the hardest-to-reach kids. Some other teachers, however, especially some of the veterans who had been there a long time and were tired and worn out, were upset about how much the kids were enjoying the lessons. Needless to say, Riley was not slowing down.

"I don't care about the pay," said Riley, which really angered the teachers' union because it didn't help their cause.

When the contract was settled, the teachers were angry at Riley. "You know this helped you, Riley. We don't want to keep looking for second and third jobs to support our family. The administration and board do not a give a darn about us."

Riley understood. But hurting kids did not turn him on.

Chapter 28

Moving Up at Work

Losing Marci Kerman, the club advisor, left a big hole for the students and staff of the school. But Riley Rossey stepped up to fill those big shoes.

Of course, Riley would continue teaching full-time and working towards his advanced degree. But this new position allowed him to work even closer with the students. And in fact, Mr. Rossey became such a student favorite that students working with counselors to form their new schedules always wanted to know what Riley was teaching.

That summer, Riley went for the entire ball of wax, working and studying. He made sure to take the maximum credits he could each session. His courses included math specialties, courses that could qualify him for credit to his future doctorate level. He also attended conferences and workshops offered by the school and the county. He was quick to learn more on his own about teaching students and how to deal with parental issues successfully.

Riley's social life was nearly zero, but he found his niche in life. Working to ensure his health was at maximum, he kept in contact with Mr. Alfred and all his men, building physical strength for the upcoming year. With his bullying days behind him, Riley turned his attention to learning more about what drove the bullies to him and what made the bullies hurt in the first place. His friendship with Juan continued as the two planned to get together for short visits.

Chapter 29

Licensed for a Future Administrative Job

After three years as a math teacher, Riley began to keep his eyes open for an administrative job. He was constantly told by his peers that he should follow in his father and grandfather's footsteps.

Riley made it known that he would like to explore possibilities not only in his school district but in others as well. He knew that even as an administrator, he would like to teach at least one class a day to stay connected one-on-one with the students. His dad and grandfather had done that through their careers and found it an invaluable experience. Besides, he had heard of too many times when administrators lost touch with the schools because they didn't see what was going on in the classrooms. As a result, they became paper pushers, office rats, or meeting ravens. They would work to find their way out of the school, attending workshops and seminars and bringing nothing back for the other teachers. "It's nice to know what other schools are doing. But talk is very cheap. Is it working? If so, how and where do the results find their way back to the administrators?"

After attending meetings in the nearby districts, Riley was able to bring back information from his many colleagues about new materials and methods. His eyes were also opened to new potential problems and possibilities as other educational veterans shared negative and positive experiences. This, for the average career seeker, may seem to be enough. But Riley also intentionally spent time with his dad, seeking to correct his mistakes and shortcomings.

Licensing is critical, so Riley was certain to complete all his necessary certifi-cations. "Those three years were such a great learning experience despite giving up my freedom and the ability to have fun. That is what a future high-ranking educator must do to serve all students." Riley continued to spend time with Mr.

Alfred, but they didn't fish and hunt as often. Instead, he was singularly focused on his goal of becoming the best possible administrator.

Chapter 30

Administrative Openings

R iley's drive and determination led him straight into a dilemma: two potential jobs he was equally excited about.

The first one was an administrative job as a full-time assistant principal in his current district. The second was a supervisor of math in his old Mason School District. Both job openings got him excited. He took into account his dad's warnings about leaving the classroom. "You have to replace yourself, and everyone wonders why you want out. Then they hold it against you, saying you are not as good as you thought you were. Of course, if you don't get a good replacement, it gets even worse. Both Grandpa and I faced the same criticism."

After much consideration, Riley decided to interview for the job at his present school. During the interview, he was asked some pretty solid questions. Of course, he was well prepared. After the interview, he was told there were two finalists; he was one. Riley, at his father's suggestion, made an appointment with the principal to get a critique of the interview. With the final interview taking place three days later, Riley wanted to make every preparation.

In his appointment with the principal, Riley shared his thoughts about what he would like to see for the students and teachers. The man who left the position had been having problems with several teachers and found himself ill-prepared for change. The principal assured Riley that his fellow teachers all liked him and respected his knowledge and preparation. They felt his students were very well prepared and respected his teaching methods. In the meeting, however, Riley found out that his competition was a veteran teacher in the school district, a highly popular athletic coach, and the superintendent's godchild. Joe Tate was his name.

Joe Tate was the favorite for the job, in Riley's opinion, for no other reason than his looks and athletic ability. Principals looking for assistants are sometimes prejudiced in favor of coaches and physical education teachers because of their disciplinary power.

So, the final interview seemed to be all about brains vs. brawn. Riley was glad to get that far and had the attitude that whatever was to happen, the process had been a great experience. According to inside information, Riley blew the interview committee out of the water. He answered questions far beyond his experience level.

The next day, Joe Tate asked to speak privately to Riley. Knowing that his godfather was in the background pushing for Joe to get the job, he told Riley not to be disappointed if he didn't get the job. "Your dad will make sure you get an administrative job, so don't get disappointed by the outcome. But, if you somehow sneak into an offer, turn it down and tell them you would rather get more experience because the guy with more experience can handle the kids better."

Riley was furious and told off Tate. "Are you kidding me? You're so worried about getting this job that you need to come here and tell me what to do?"

Tate responded, "It's up to you. But when I get this job, I can make your life miserable, or you can have a successful career."

Riley considered his words carefully and then left Tate with a thought. "I feel bad for you that you think you can bully me one way or another. So take this with you: I have learned much from two generations of principals that a jock like you as an assistant principal thinks only about power over teaching. Now, get out of my class so I can prepare for my trigonometry lesson. Or would you like to try to teach my lesson while I hand out basketballs, blow my whistle, and play fantasy league during class time?"

Tate slammed the door and took off.

After three interviews, Tate got the job. Riley thanked the principal. "With all respect, I know I have qualities you can't teach. If I had been your choice, your job would have become much easier, and our work together would have reached a more professional level." The principal looked at Riley, not sure what he meant.

That year, Riley was the favorite for Teacher of the Year in his school district. However, a veteran teacher beat him out. Riley graciously said, "Well deserved," even though many people thought that Riley was the one who should have been chosen. This was just another mature statement from Riley on learning how to treat winners.

After spending a year with Mr. Tate, Riley and other staff members agreed: Mr. Tate was a very unsure assistant principal who was inconsistent with the students, not respected by parents, and not a great resource when teachers needed him.

An unfortunate accident occurred at the end of the school year: a tree fell on Mr. Tate's car while he was driving. He was injured and would be unable to work indefinitely. This created a temporary opening for his job.

Chapter 31

Mason School District Seeks a Math Supervisor

Over the summer, Riley found out that the Mason School district math supervisor job had reopened. This intrigued him as he was very sentimental about living through his grandfather and father's past and becoming the third generation of Rossey administrators.

Dr. Richard Rossey and Riley had a long conversation. Mr. Davis, Riley's ultimate bully, was still in the school district where there was an opening. Even though the opening was at the high school, Dr. Rossey was very leery of the sneaky Mr. Davis, who, like the entire Davis family, was likely still holding a grudge.

Despite this, Riley decided he would apply. At the same time, his own administration requested that he fill in for Mr. Tate during his rehabilitation—a position that would likely last 4-5 months.

Riley was granted an interview with the search committee at Mason, which went great. Some staff members recognized Riley and cheered his answers and his personality. Mr. Alfred had a little bit of say, which was respected by many of the teachers who knew the relationship the two men had while Riley was in the Mason District.

So Riley had a tough decision. Should he stick with the school he was with, filling in at a higher level, or would he actually get a chance to be in his old district? The politics were running wild. As suspected, Mr. Davis began bad-mouthing the Rosseys and telling anyone who would listen, "You will regret hiring this wimpy kid."

Another teacher at the middle school, however, was elated. He publicly voiced that Riley was one of the best students he ever had in his 30 years at the school. As Riley processed, he told his friend, Mr. Alfred, "This would be a great opportunity for me to work with some excellent teachers at the high school. I would be able to help kids overcome what I had to."

Mr. Alfred, still positioned at the high school, confirmed Riley's thoughts. "The boys all know you, and the new guys know your story. They will be watching closely."

The committee announced that they whittled the pool down to two candidates: Riley and a veteran from another school district. The questions during the next interview were detailed. One of the interviewers, who knew how much Riley was bullied when he attended the school, asked the obvious: "Have you conquered your problem with being bullied?"

Rather than putting the blame on others, Riley responded, "I was just as responsible for the incidents. My behavior needed to be reshaped, and I have done it. My main concern is to use the experience to keep others from making the same mistakes. Not every student will succeed by my formula, but I'm sure I can help them."

He vividly presented what he had done and would continue to do. The answer brought smiles and raves from two committee members, and one board member shouted, "Don't let Mr. Rossey get away."

The process for his interview was nearly over when one of the staff members on the committee asked about his relationship with Mr. Davis.

"I don't have anything negative to say about Mr. Davis. I have grown to be a responsible son, teacher, and a man on a mission to be the best person I can be. If I am asked to work closely with him, I will not have a problem with that. I will respect him and his position."

The next day, Dr. Rossey was told that his son's interview went great but that his competition was stiff because the other candidate had much more experience.

Riley waited several days to learn the decision. He knew his interview went well. His other school was still leaning on him to fill in as assistant principal until Mr. Tate returned and sweetened the pot by telling him he was on the list for a supervisor or administrative job.

After waiting for what seemed like forever, Riley was asked by the Mason District supervisor to come to his office to meet with several committee members. There, they told him they had given him the highest possible evaluation, higher than any other they had ever given a teaching candidate. With excitement, they continued, "We expect more promotions for you in the future."

The committee was elated when Mr. Riley Rossey accepted the position of math supervisor in the Mason School District.

Riley was thrilled. But the parents and faculty at the school where he had grown so much and now would soon be leaving were feeling bittersweet.

Chapter 32

LEARNING ABOUT HIS NEW SUPERVISOR POSITION

Riley was ready for the challenge of supervising and teaching. He began by spending a lot of time getting to know the students, staff, parents, and the curriculum. At first, it seemed very strange that he often talked to people he knew when he had attended high school there. The staff was very supportive—many long-term staff members remembered him. But they also recalled how, in high school, Riley rose above many of his middle school problems.

Riley ensured the staff had input for the math department's short and long-term goals. And the staff wanted to ensure Riley was aware of the department's pressing needs. Riley was a good listener and took notes.

Jerry Rhome had been a teacher for over thirty years and knew Riley well. He was pleased with the long way Riley had come since being a student in the school and was very supportive.

Dan Wieskoff, on the other hand, worked at the elementary school and did not get along with Riley's dad. Part of the reason was that his evaluations were always lousy, but so was his performance as a teacher. Mr. Wieskoff's dislike of Dr. Rossey carried over to feelings for Riley. However, he was in the minority.

Dr. Rossey had a staff meeting to clear the air, and it was very successful. "Mr. Wieskoff, you are one of several teachers who have a problem returning phone calls to parents." Dr. Rossey was fuming when parents called him directly with complaints about the lack of returned calls and poor communication between parents and teachers. "If you can be more attentive to that detail, I'm sure we will get along better."

Another teacher, Ms. Marcinski, asked for a private meeting with Riley. She didn't like second-hand information and wanted to make sure Riley was going to be an asset to the staff. At the end of their meeting, she was very satisfied with the answers and thanked Riley for his time.

Riley decided he would teach two classes—one very high-level math course and one remedial math course. Although the principal wanted him to teach only one class, Riley explained, "I want to teach the remedial class so I can relate to what teachers have to go through with some of our more difficult students."

Riley did the obvious research. He reviewed teachers' past evaluations, students' test scores, and improvement plans for the staff. He even interviewed some students to get their opinions on how their class year went. This brought quite a bit of controversy as information on what students felt about their teachers did not go over well with teacher associations.

Riley quickly learned about some issues. Certain teachers with poor reputations blamed the students, the parents' lack of support, or even the supplies they had available to them. The list went on and on and on. They blamed anything but their own attention to teaching.

The more Riley heard from some of those teachers, the more he could hear his dad and grandfather saying, "Excuses, excuses, excuses."

Riley devised a system of giving extra credit to advanced students for tutoring other students. This helped not only those who were struggling with math but also gave further learning opportunities to those who became mentors.

"People want solutions put into effect immediately. Since what we have is not working, what are we waiting for? For students to leave without the necessary skills for the next level is unacceptable."

One of Riley's hot-button issues was any staff not getting back to parents within twenty-four hours. He recognized that many parents work and their time is valuable. He also knew that calls to a teacher regarding a student, whether because of an academic issue or other problem, are usually time-sensitive. Having lived through bullying incidents, Riley understood how important it is that parents' questions be addressed in a timely manner. "Everyone makes mistakes, but the key is how fast you address and correct those mistakes."

Riley also told the staff that meeting face-to-face with staff and students was a priority. "Writing memos and sending written reprimands is not a good way to operate. Certainly, follow-up memos are needed in some cases and should be kept in records. But trust is easier to attain when difficult topics are addressed face-to-face."

With poor results, the last supervisor had operated by memos alone and rarely had face-to-face meetings. Riley knew it would be challenging for the staff to change their protocol. "Give the staff some good constructive criticism and time to fix it. It's okay to make a mistake or more. It is not okay to let something that does not work for the students go on and on."

One teacher, Mr. Eggeth, had spent 30 years at the same school teaching the same classes. Through an informal review and speaking to the principal, Riley realized he hadn't changed his lesson plan for decades. According to Mr. Eggeth, he's a great teacher and motivator. He was also very close to several board members. But although his evaluations had been just satisfactory, Mr. Eggeth had never been challenged to grow in his field. Riley made a note to have him teach a different level math class the following year.

A few weeks into the school year, Riley became more concerned when a parent called and said her child was having problems with Mr. Eggeth. The statement supposedly to the student from Mr. Eggeth was, "Is your parent still waiting for checks to come in the mail? If so, it must mean you are training for the same future since you don't get your work done."

Riley immediately questioned him, "Why would you say that about a parent?"

"Well, I have had the family members for the last ten years, and it's always the same. Years ago, before you came, I had all the meetings, all the documentation that I needed. I was told I did everything right, and the Planter lady was a bad parent who had all these kids, no husband, and no support from anyone."

Riley's next step was to sit with Mr. Eggeth, Ms. Planter, and her son Thomas, one of her four children.

Prior to the conference, Mr. Eggeth did not say hello to Ms. Planter, nor did he introduce her to Mr. Rossey, to whom he said, "I don't really need you to be at this conference, but you're the boss, so be my guest." Mr. Eggeth did not even pull the student out of class to attend the conference.

Riley took note of all this, recognizing Mr. Eggeth's attitude and comments as a problem.

Mr. Rossey, allowing Mr. Eggeth to run the conference, listened as he did not have a good word to say about Thomas. Ms. Planter never smiled, did not ask any questions, or was asked how the school could help Thomas. The conference lasted ten minutes. The parent was not escorted out or thanked for her attendance.

"Do you see what I'm dealing with?" asked Mr. Eggeth. Riley was flabbergasted. "I've had too much experience with this parent to let her take over. By the way, I have a homebound instruction, so if we need to continue this conversation, it has to be another time." Mr. Eggeth then thanked Riley for the support, got up from the conference table, and walked out. He did not even say goodbye.

Riley reviewed the conference with his supervisor, who told him he was barking up the wrong tree. "Mr. Eggeth has been that way for years. No one wants to touch him with a twenty-foot pole. If you want to go after this, I will support you. But I guarantee you that somewhere down the line, this will all go away. Mr. Eggeth will survive. However, you may not."

Riley called his dad, who was familiar with the Eggeth situation. He knew the politics, but Riley was determined to stop Mr. Eggeth from keeping students from succeeding. So, after discussing the matter with his dad, Riley became determined to either change Mr. Eggeth's behavior or hold him accountable.

Riley met with Mr. Eggeth and Thomas. The big question was, did Thomas recognize a problem? Riley proposed bringing back Mrs. Planter and making a plan for Thomas to get extra help at home, either from his mom or a sibling. Also, he tasked Mr. Eggeth with pairing Thomas up with a buddy in class who could help him keep up.

Of course, the success of the plan was up to Mr. Eggeth, whose response to Riley was, "You're the supervisor, but you're wasting your time."

At that point, Riley decided it was time to be the aggressor. So the match was on, and it started getting nasty. Several teachers quietly told Riley, "It's about time someone has the nerve to go after Eggeth." And "George Eggeth is not a good teacher, trust me," said one fellow teacher in confidence.

Many staff members wondered if Riley would pay for confronting Eggeth. Surprisingly, Mr. Eggeth was not concerned—but he did announce he would be retiring at the end of the year. That did not deter Riley from closely monitoring and evaluating him.

As the school year progressed, it became well-known that Riley was the bad guy, forcing a veteran teacher into retirement. But many staff disagreed. Not a word—of either concern or praise—came from the board members when they accepted his retirement. Riley's dad was very proud, not about the retirement per se, but about the fact Riley had sought accountability. "By the way, George Eggeth is very popular with several of our golfers," said his dad.

Riley found himself dealing with other issues. One was teachers who would allow students to be late for class without any repercussions. One day, Riley stood in front of Mr. Batson's class, watching students enter the class late without even a look from the teacher. Mr. Batson was at the chalkboard as the students walked right by him to sit in their seats. At first, Riley thought, okay, maybe the teacher did not want to interrupt his thought process. Maybe he would wait until the end of the period to say something. But Mr. Batson never said a word.

Riley had never been a "gotcha" type of person. His dad had firmly trained him never to be that way. But he dropped a note to Mr. Batson, asking him to stop in and see him at the end of the school day. "Bill, why didn't you say a word to the students who were late for your class today?"

"Well, I gave them a zero for the day. And I make it a point at the beginning of the school year to let the class know my rule."

When Riley sat down with the principal at the end of the day to discuss the matter, her response really made Riley even more concerned. "Listen, Riley, Batson has a direct line to the school superintendent, and everyone knows that, so they don't mess with him. He's a decent teacher. So we worry about the bigger problems."

Five years prior, two math teachers in Riley's department had begun dating. Two years after that, they had gotten married. During the time they dated, they were both considered excellent teachers. Every supervisor and administrator left it at that. But in the next three years, their lives entered turmoil.

First, the Freightners had family issues with Barbara's parents. Then, they had a child who was often ill, which meant one of the two parents had to stay home. In addition, the grandparents lived out of state and had their own problems, which overflowed to the young couple, limiting their availability to work. Something had to give in their lives, and it was their teaching that suffered. At various points, Riley had to have conferences with the two individually. He would also take on either one of their classes when an emergency happened, causing one of them to run home. But that was a band-aid.

Riley held a meeting with both teachers, the principal, and the two assistant principals, trying to iron out the difficulties. Brainstorming together, they all decided to put an excellent math teacher, who had recently retired and wanted to substitute teach, on call. This would lessen the impact of their absences.

This solution helped the teachers feel less stressed. And after some adjustments in their lives, both resumed being the excellent teachers they had been. This greatly benefitted the students and made the school and department run so much more effectively. Rightly, Riley was given much of the credit for this victory. Prior to his steady and level-headed involvement, it wasn't unusual for the district to bash teachers going through a life crisis, negatively affecting the entire environment.

Chapter 33

Issues with Other Teachers and Grades

Some of the issues Riley had with teachers centered around grading and notifying parents. Although email makes it easy to communicate, some variables had to be addressed. For example, was it necessary and appropriate for teachers to spend time at night communicating with parents and students? Do parents want to be on a computer or phone with a teacher after a day at work? And regarding grades, when was it necessary to contact parents if a student was getting a bad grade? When was it appropriate? Though circumstances were unique, Riley made it mandatory that each teacher had a method to keep track of each parent's preferred method of contact.

And then there was the question of what happens if a teacher gives the student a grade they don't deserve. Just as teachers needed a way to contact the parents, so the parents needed to know how to best contact the teacher. So it became mandatory for each teacher to address this matter specifically.

Riley became famous, or some may say infamous, for some of the quotes he repeated over and over:

- "You need to call the parent back within 24 hours."

- "Why are we allowing small problems to become big problems?"

- "Do we need an act of Congress to make this work?"

- "Call the parents as many times and as often as necessary so we don't have a problem."

- "We don't want to get egg on our faces and be accused of a lack of follow-up."

Riley did his best and ran a tight ship. But it wasn't long before he was threatened by the veteran teacher who said, "Now I know why you were bullied when you were in school. You were a pain in the neck to other kids, and you were scared when you were threatened."

Well, as Riley was no longer about being bullied, he went for the jugular. He wrote a letter directly about that teacher—one that stated facts based on everything flagged in his file that others had been afraid to bring into the light. And, rather than mail it to anyone, Riley handed a copy of the letter directly to that teacher and waited for his response, which was, "My union representative and my attorney will address this."

After that, the teacher became scarce, avoiding Riley and walking a straight path. No union representative or attorney ever came forward.

Chapter 34

Down Goes an Administrator

One morning, Riley woke up to a phone call from his principal. One of the assistant principals had a serious illness that would require surgery, forcing him to miss four to five months of work. This put the school in a bind as there were no funds available in the budget for additional staff. So, the principal had decided that the best measure would be to ask an existing staff member to take the position on a stipend basis. As Riley had experience and aspired to move up the ranks, the principal had decided he was an excellent candidate.

He did want Riley to consider the offer carefully, as the position required someone with disciplinarian experience. And though Riley's past as a bullied kid would help qualify him, it could also make him apprehensive. And, with all Riley was doing, the administration certainly didn't want him chewing off any more than he could handle.

After getting a vote of confidence from his dad and several staff members, Riley began to get excited about the opportunity.

Then he got a surprise text from James Davis, who said, "Call me if you need me. And don't be scared of the high school bullies."

"Yeah, right," Riley muttered under his breath. Though he had managed to steer clear of Mr. Davis, he had heard through the grapevine that Mr. Davis was totally against the move. But that text? It somehow made Riley more confident than ever.

So, suddenly, Riley's list of responsibilities grew. He was the math supervisor over several older teachers who couldn't be fired thanks to tenure; an assistant principal in charge of 1000 11th and 12th graders; and he taught a low-level class of freshmen with many math deficiencies and a high-level class with the brightest students in the school.

Add all that to the college courses Riley was taking for his doctorate and his tutoring of college students in the morning and high school students after school—at 25 years of age, Riley had more responsibility than he should have. His parents began to wonder when he would sleep.

Not only that, many students' parents remembered Riley as a scared elementary or middle school kid and questioned his level of responsibility. Most of the staff decided Riley got the job because, with such a low-paying stipend, nobody else wanted it.

Still, Riley was confident as he continued to be on the lookout for students like him who needed heavy-duty counseling and support. That was why he had returned to work in the education system in the first place.

It wasn't long before a former classmate of Riley's came to school to complain about several students harassing his son in math class. Mr. Wilson said, "I hope you can handle this better than you handled school when you were bullied." Riley's response blew him away.

"I will talk to your son alone, then with you and your wife present. I want you to come to me immediately if this problem arises again. I will take immediate action and have you, a counselor, and the other students' parents in a meeting. I will also talk privately with the teacher; you will be notified of my meeting results."

"If the student who is bullying Mark looks at him the wrong way, he will not return to class. He will be moved to another class and warned that I will recommend suspension, home instruction, or a transfer to another high school. If any of his friends are accomplices, they will pay a price, which I will tell them to their faces. I will not let this go for one minute until the problem is solved to my satisfaction."

"If I have to, I will bring in the police, charge the student with harassment, and bring him and his dad to the Board of Education for review."

The father was flabbergasted by this whole approach. The word in the school went viral that Mr. Rossey was not the same person he was when he was a student.

Riley said afterward, "I would probably like to have shadowed the assistant principal before I accepted this job, but there was no time."

Riley had no problem with being in charge. He took daily walks around the building every morning and after school. His presence brought respectful silence when he entered classrooms, the cafeteria, gym locker rooms, and even bathrooms. Of course, he was always welcome in the custodians and maintenance office. And he would often bring his lunch to eat with the maintenance staff, while keeping his phone active.

Besides his walks in the building, Riley did something no other administrator did: surprise patrolling the student parking lot in the morning, between classes, and even after school. After chasing students out, he spoke to the principal about possible drug sales and drug use in the lot, who responded, "Look, we have enough problems without us getting into the parking lot."

Riley couldn't believe what he heard. So one day, his surprise visit brought a bigger surprise. One of the students was sitting in his car with a bag of what appeared to be marijuana. Riley immediately called the principal, who told him to call the police. The student froze as the police told him to get out of the vehicle. It seems like this young man was getting ready to sell several pounds of drugs to students.

That time, Riley ran into a very cooperative parent as his son was taken away in handcuffs. What followed was the principal's suggestion. She wanted to take the credit for raiding the parking lot in the morning, and forty-seven students who did not get the message were suspended from school. At Riley's suggestion, they each had to bring their parents in before being readmitted to school. No phone calls. "If they don't come in person, their son or daughter will remain suspended."

One parent, insisting that a phone call would be sufficient, said she couldn't come in as she leaves for work at 6:00 am. Riley replied, "I'll meet you at 5:30 am in the main building."

At 5:30, the parent, who was a Board of Education member and a medical official in the community, arrived and was livid. Riley explained, "Your daughter was in the parking lot with another student and was smoking in her car."

"My daughter doesn't smoke."

"You know, if your daughter had been in the parking lot studying, I would have let her go."

At that, the woman used language that Riley would not repeat.

But then the mother asked her daughter what had happened. The daughter replied by calling Mr. Rossey a bitch and admitting to smoking with her boyfriend, Billy, whom the parents did not permit her to speak with.

The parent was appalled and thanked Riley for his caring and actions to keep the students safe and honest.

After three days of patrolling the parking lot, nobody was hanging out. However, someone wrote on the pavement, "Rosy sucks."

The principal and Riley's father congratulated him on being respected by the student body.

"I'm really annoyed," said Riley. "He spelled my name 'Rosy.'"

After checking with a couple of snitches, Riley found out who the vandal was and had him clean the graffiti along with the rest of the parking lot.

Another day, Riley was told that there were complaints about vehicles going through the bus zone, some at high speed. One parent asked if Riley was going to do something about this dangerous behavior. First, he assigned one of the school resource police to keep a close watch on the bus area. Then, he decided to sit near the bus zone area as he did some of his other work, such as grading papers and answering emails.

The students thought Riley was crazy as he sat outside with a makeshift desk. But when a car went zooming through the bus zone, ignoring all signs, Riley caught the model and the license plate of the vehicle. Then, the driver parked his vehicle at the end of the zone and walked into the building.

Riley confronted the parent as he handed a pair of sneakers to his son by the gym door. Riley could not wait to find out why this parent couldn't do what everyone does: park in a designated parking space and come in through the main office.

When Riley approached him, Mr. Lewis was surprised and apologized for not thinking. He then thanked Riley for paying attention to such an important security issue. This situation caused the school to review its outdoor security plans more carefully.

The principal decided to write an accommodation to Riley's file and thank him for paying attention to details. Realizing that Riley was doing so much, she asked to see a schedule of his typical day in order to determine how he could reduce some of his responsibilities. So Riley spelled it out.

RILEY'S SCHEDULE

6:00 am – Workout in the school gym and do a check of the building

7:15 am – Check phone messages on his cell and school phone; check emails

7:45 am – Meet with staff as needed

8:00 am – Greet students at the front door

8:45 am – Check out the morning breakfast program in the cafeteria (Riley believed he and the counselors and other personnel should be going to the kids, not just waiting on them. Riley had a portable table by the school cafeteria and was able to talk directly to the students. He did not believe it was necessary to pull the kids out of class and make them miss valuable teaching.)

9:00 am – Teach a class

9:50 am – Examine discipline forms submitted by teachers (If they are not detailed or do not include follow-up calls, send them back to the teacher)

10:15 am – Walk through the math classes and address department issues.

11:00 am – Walk through bathrooms, lunch room, and non-visible areas outside the lunchroom to make sure there are no illegal activities; check out the parking when not covered by the resource police

RILEY'S SCHEDULE (cont.)

11:45 am – Visit with the custodians to review any concerns regarding maintenance or students defacing property

12:30 pm – Prepare for class; grab a bite to eat

1:00 pm – Teach second class

1:50 pm – Meet with students who need discipline reviews; meet with teachers.

2:30 pm – Meet with support staff to address concerns (Riley was very well-liked by his support staff. Because of his busy schedule, they jokingly gave him a scooter so he could get around. Of course, he never used it.)

3:00 pm – Prepare for dismissal; supervise buses, parking lots, and be in touch with resource officers and teachers on duty.

3:30 pm – Meet with staff as needed and attend meetings; check after-school activities; make sure no unsupervised students are in the building.

4:15 pm – Complete evaluations and other reports

5:45 pm – Review doctorate coursework, teaching lessons, college course

9:00 pm – Read and review work for the next day

10:30 pm – Lights out, go to sleep

Of course, Riley was very flexible should an unforeseen incident happen or other changes be needed.

Somehow, Riley's schedule leaked to other administrators, leaving their mouths wide open. And when Mr. Davis saw it, he was royally upset. "This guy is going to cause us problems. They will want us all to work as hard as he does." He figured the only way to prevent himself from having to work any bit harder than he was would be to seek the presidency of the administrators' association. That turned out to be very easy because no one wanted that job. But to his surprise, he got the title without pay, which made him angry. Angry once again at Rossey, who was always causing him trouble.

Chapter 35

Dealing with the Teacher Association

Riley maintained that he did not get into education to go on work stoppages. "If I wanted to get into the money world, I would focus only on making money." He was a little annoyed with the teachers' association because they mainly concentrated on money, the weaker teachers were the most vocal members, and they considered themselves a union to look more powerful. Then, when one of the leaders had a confrontation with a student, Riley wondered about the virtues of the group.

Riley received a call from a teacher saying a student would not listen and was causing a major disturbance in class. When Riley arrived, he saw a student standing in the corner of the room with his hands folded and looking angry.

The teacher reiterated that Marty, a student-athlete, would not take his hat off and would not listen to the teacher. Riley knew Marty and had a good relationship with him, so he asked him to come out of the room so they could talk. Once there, Riley asked Marty what had happened.

"The teacher screamed at me and told me to take the hat off, or I would get an F for the day." With thirty students in a high school class, Riley knew that kind of tactic did not work very well.

Then, the worst embarrassment for the student came when the teacher told him he would call his mom and write up a detailed misconduct form. Riley knew the student's mother had passed away several years ago, and he was living with his aunt. He was livid that the teacher did not bother to look at records or have any information about the student before he went to him.

Marty then apologized, took off his hat, and gave it to Riley, who then sent him back to class, telling him he should come see him after school to get his hat. Riley also kiddingly said that if the student didn't come, he would sell the hat. Marty laughed. And Riley told him, "Just go sit down in your seat and don't respond."

At the end of the day, the teacher came to see Riley with a three-page misconduct form written out blow by blow. "How long will he be suspended?" asked the teacher.

"He won't be," Riley replied, explaining that there were missteps on both sides.

Next thing you know, the teacher submitted a grievance against Riley. Of course, that teacher was the vice president of the teachers' association. Every morning, when he walked into work, he would take 5-10 blank misconduct forms, anticipating problems with students. Riley decided to make the forms not so readily available. After that, teachers who wanted the forms had to ask Riley for them. Ironically, some of the best teachers did not know the form existed.

Riley's dad gave him an earful on teachers' associations. He said, "You know what? Your friend, Mr. Alfred, was asked if his people ever have problems with students. His first answer did not surprise anyone. 'Are you kidding me? Are you on drugs?' Then he said, 'NO. If we have a problem, we take care of it quickly, sometimes even by going to the student's home after school—most of my guys and gals live in the neighborhood.' I see the way some of your teachers talk to the students. If it was me in my heyday, I would either give some of these teachers a dirty look or have my dad come and threaten to kick the stuffing out of them."

Putting more parameters in place, Riley required a teacher who had a substantial problem with a student to notify the parent with a phone call. He also gave every teacher permission to signal Riley to take over the class if things needed cooling and offered to arrange a meeting with any student before the end of the day.

Chapter 36

Visit from the State Education Department

Riley and his dad always suggested that each day, staff should imagine and prepare for the possibility that the state department supervisors would be coming in to monitor the schools. That would prevent the mad scramble of getting ready on short notice to put on a show just to be approved when they did come. Mr. Alfred and many teachers were always prepared. However, other teachers had a problem with the way the school was run and would rather complain than work to make things better.

The principal warned everyone to always be on their best behavior, making sure their required paperwork and room were at their best. Riley agreed. "Just make sure you are at your best every day, then you won't ever have to worry about who comes in your class." Riley suggested a mock monitoring day at the beginning of the year and a monthly meeting to enforce this thought.

One month, on the same evening as the monitoring meeting, Riley also had a pre-scheduled doctorate meeting. The superintendent would not give any leniency, even for those seeking advanced education, and required Riley's attendance. "Your job is your number one priority." Fortunately, Riley's supervisor at the university was very cooperative and allowed the doctorate meeting to be rescheduled.

Of course, Mr. Davis made his thoughts well known. "I can't believe Rossey would even suggest not cooperating. But that's Rossey for you."

Riley's dad responded, "The school should be proud Riley is seeking a higher education. Mr. Davis needs college refresher courses since he somehow became an administrator without the necessary advanced degree. But he never has a reason to improve himself or his staff—because he knows it all."

Chapter 37

The Principal Goes Down

Can lighting strike twice in the same school district? I guess so because the principal went down after an accident, which sent him out of work for two months. So the assistant principals divvied up the principal's responsibilities. And, as Riley was the last person hired, most of the duties were added to his list, making his days even longer. But Riley's attitude remained so positive and motivating that no one knew just how hard he was working.

The teachers at the high school were a mixed bag. Some wanted blood from the kids, and others had no problem with dealing "the hand they were dealt." Despite their attitude, their main asset was that Riley had far exceeded their expectations for support. He just always handled any concerns quicker than you could imagine. The fact that he had the backs of both the professionals and the paraprofessionals made the staff very confident.

Riley did not always agree with everyone and sometimes needed to negotiate with staff, students, and parents, but he was really good at seeing all sides and looking out for everyone. As a result, the great teachers became better, and the average teachers moved their game up. His staff members gained more confidence in themselves and in Riley as a leader.

Of course, Mr. Davis, at the middle school, heard all the good things but still warned others, "Watch your back for Rossey."

Riley sent some suggestions to modify school procedures after consulting with his fellow administrators and staff, and they actually seemed to be working.

Chapter 38

SPECIAL PROGRAMS FOR INDIVIDUAL STUDENTS

Innovation was always on Riley's mind, no matter the program. He was sensitive to the challenged students and those who spoke English as a second language. He was always aware of any student going through the same struggles he had gone through. And he was especially concerned with making sure the teaching staff had the proper training, which would give the students the best opportunity to succeed.

Riley always listened to the plans of staff, regardless of where they came from. Sending teachers to other programs outside the district was always a plus for the teaching staff. Even paraprofessionals could attend conferences if it helped them or if it helped other staff.

One of Riley's plans to help staff continually improve was to pay them to attend advanced education programs after school and during the summer. Riley would get annoyed whenever anyone spoke of using the summer to relax and get away from students. Yes, family time is important, but so is keeping sharp and not forgetting the information that you have learned. Like his father, Riley always asked his teachers to come up with ideas that would help them not have their skills become stale.

As the school year ended and other administrators returned, Riley's days got a bit shorter. He was very appreciative for the opportunity he received.

Chapter 39

FAMILIAR INFORMATION AT A SYMPOSIUM

Riley was finally finishing his coursework for his doctorate degree. The title and subject were very appropriate. "What would a bullied student do if he was one day in charge of the school?" His university mentor and advisor asked him to speak at summer symposiums discussing that subject, among other important points. Riley prepared well, knowing he would be asked many questions. He was quite ready after his extensive research. Several hundred parents, teachers, and college students would be present at the conferences.

Riley was called upon as one of the guest speakers to give a synopsis of his educational experience. Here is some of what he presented.

"Successful students often have engaged and successful parents. Parenting is a 24/7 job that includes not only caring for the child but also teaching and guiding them. When issues occur, we would do well as a society not to look for a place to lay blame—other students, parents, the school system, the environment, or just bad luck—but to look for a solution."

"It is a fact of life that there are bullies who hurt others. I was bullied as a child. Until I learned that it was my responsibility to find a solution to the problem, nothing changed. Despite my heartache and my parents' hard work, they couldn't fix the situation. I finally realized I was part of the problem; therefore, I could be the largest part of the solution. I was a scared kid, socially well below my chronological age while academically above. Thank goodness I had an angel. He was a man you would never expect to be my best friend. Many saw him as just a maintenance man. Wow, he could probably have run the school with no college credits. Having come from a fishing and hunting family, you could see he had what no one could teach him."

"He was brilliant, pragmatic, had a great feel for people, and was always there when I needed him. He would never think of letting anyone down. He could fix any machinery in or outside of the school. He would look at my mistakes and help me correct them immediately. He was one in twenty million, and he was there for me. We even became best friends outside of school. He is still there for me, always has my back, and isn't afraid to kick my butt when I need it. The kick in the butt is for discipline, by the way, not child abuse. I'm speaking about Mr. Archie Alfred."

"After going to college, returning to the school system where I was bullied was the last place on earth I wanted to be. Although my parents said a long time ago that this was my destiny, it finally took my college roommate to convince me. I decided I would follow in the footsteps of my grandpa and dad."

"So let's look at what parents, teachers, and communities can be aware of to prevent kids like me from falling prey to and succumbing to the power of bullies. Here are some very important points I've learned from experience and from others that I'd like to pass on to you:

- Consistency at home is important.

- When children do something wrong, they should be confronted.

- Taking time to recognize what a child is dealing with is crucial. If you are a parent, the fact that you have two jobs is not your kid's fault.

- Kids want to understand. It's important to have a valid response when a child asks why they can't do certain things adults do.

- We can help kids learn what they don't know on the social scene while we teach them to respect each other for who they are.

- A school can help identify medical services that may help a child, but parents are responsible for seeking and paying for the care.

- Both the teacher and the parent can be instrumental in helping a child with a problem.

- There are resources to help single parents.

- Parents aren't perfect. Neither are teachers. We should all do the best we can and not blame each other.

- Being a parent and a teacher are both relational positions. It's okay to lean on each other.

- It is just as important to praise a child when he makes good decisions as to discipline him when he doesn't.

- We all have strengths and weaknesses. Students, parents, and teachers.

- A problem that happens in a neighborhood or a friend circle on the weekend can affect children in school on Monday. Adults should be aware and be willing to step in.

- A child becomes an adult at 18 years old. Families should plan accordingly.

- Raising a child takes a lot of care and work from many in the community."

"Students recognize hypocritical teachers faster than anyone. Teachers must respect students if they expect students to respect them. But it is also important to teach children that, while a ten-year-old child is not the boss over a thirty-year-old, they shouldn't be bullied by them either. And yes, it is possible for a child to be bullied by a teacher."

"The bottom line is that we all hold the responsibility to see, listen to, and guide each of the children in our care to the best of our abilities. We must each work tirelessly as the future of our society depends on the strength of our youth."

Riley finished speaking to roaring applause and then took questions. Each question became a discussion that led to positive comments.

Single parenting was one topic that Riley spent time discussing. "I'm a single parent, and my 13-year-old is bigger and stronger than me. He wakes up in the middle of the night and leaves the house."

"Stop right there," said Riley. "Where do you think that he's going?"

"He won't tell me. And when I try to stop him, he pushes me away."

"It sounds like it's time for you to tell him you are calling the police."

"That seems drastic. And I don't want him to have a police record."

"His safety is your main concern. Most police have counseling training to deal with these problems. It is not safe for a thirteen-year-old to be out of his house at 3 am."

Riley continued, turning from the individual parent to the crowd. "Sometimes giving necessary discipline is difficult, but it is essential. I remember a teacher I had in school who had no control over the class. One day, he came in and said, 'Okay, anyone who does not sit in their assigned seat or talks out of turn will get sent to the principal's office.'"

"The laughter was so loud that the teacher felt defeated and just continued teaching even though the students were not listening. Some of the strongest parents I have seen are single parents who are small in size but are some of the meanest hombres, who, though they never hit a child, commanded respect."

"When you run into a problem with your child, seek wisdom. Ask your parents or your grandparents what they would do. They will likely tell you to run a tighter ship. Parenting and teaching are very demanding jobs that many of us have relaxed into. Remember when you were growing up and the kitchen was your parents' responsibility? If you didn't eat a meal when it was mealtime, you had to wait to eat. The kitchen was not open 24-hours."

"It's important to assess where you are in your life with your kids, and if you are a teacher, to be aware of what the student may be going through at home. Every family is different and all families face problems, whether one or both parents work, if the home has a single parent, extended family, stepchildren, or several children living with a father, mother, or foster parent. Homes today sometimes consist of gay parents living together, an older adult-age-sibling raising the kids, or grandparents struggling to take care of themselves and several children on a retirement income. Whatever the situation, we as adults must adjust and respond to the needs of the child who is growing physically, socially, and emotionally. That takes love and discipline."

"Remember when grandma had the broom, the shoe, or the belt laid out on the floor, and that was enough to scare the daylights out of you? That was called discipline. Today, using those things is called child abuse. I am not a fan by any means of hitting a child. There are so many resources today that were not available in the past. Dealing with mental illness, drug abuse, and alcoholism without getting help has become our biggest problem."

The next question that came from the audience was interesting. "Why do certain parents get what they want out of the school and others cannot?"

"That's a very good question," said Riley. "Listen, my parents were heard loud and clear when I was bullied, whether or not the staff responded. But today, I demand that staff respond to parents within 24 hours of them reaching out, or I will be on their case. Administrators must hold teachers to that. There are teachers who want to get the almighty tenure and just can't wait until that happens. Remember the spoil system. Better known as 'one hand washes the other. Take care of my kid, and I'll take of you. Contribute to my reelection, and I'll take care of you.' The bottom line is that even with all our rules, regulations, and laws, people still get away with so much."

"Do you know there are days that certain teachers write reams of discipline reports when something goes wrong in the classroom? They would never talk directly to a parent or child. So what's the answer for a parent? KEEP GOING in a very professional way until you get what you want. It may not happen right away, but you have the responsibility to take care of your child."

Next, one parent asked, "Two of my children are very small in stature and get picked on by bigger bullies. How can I stop that?"

"I certainly can relate to being bullied. But you know, I saw students who were small in stature and couldn't figure out why they were not being picked on like I was. Were they paying off the bullies? Did they have a brother or sister who was big and strong threatening them? Was it my job to make sure I was not wearing fly paper and attracting them? Although any of those might be true, in my case, I had to take responsibility to solve the issue."

"Remember this: Physical size and gender don't always mean something. Remember David and Goliath? Bullies decide who they are going to leave alone and who they are not. We, as a society, must stand against bullying. Teachers should take charge, parents should help instill confidence, and your child must decide to move forward toward their goals—despite who or what comes against them. When teachers are backed by administrators, when parents show love, and when bullies are disciplined, then the bullied can stand tall and be comfortable becoming who they were created to be."

"I remember a teacher I had who was no more than five feet tall. The kids knew she was supporting them, and they supported her. If any student tried to test her, the class did not let the person get away with it. Often, when we all lean on and stand up for each other, the problems lessen. Next question?"

"What do I do if my kid is 18 years old and says, 'I'm an adult now?'"

Riley responded, "So, legally, there are certain rights that an 18-year-old does have. I suggest you give him or her the test: Who pays the rent? Who buys the food? Who washes the dirty clothes? Who pays for the car insurance? You may, of course, add your own questions. And when you run up against the attitude your 18-year-old might hold of not calling you when he gets in trouble, you can always ask a similar question: Who pays for more than half your support? So now, you, as a parent, can determine what kind of kid you have: the one who respects you or one who thinks you're his peer. Sometimes, an 18-year-old is an independent, cooperative adult who is actually living on their own. As a parent, you must adjust."

Another woman raised her hand, "What happens when there is a problem in the neighborhood causing my kid not to want to go to school?"

Riley replied, "Please notify the school so we are aware of the problem. Notify us before the problem gets bigger and bigger. You may even find it beneficial to contact community resources or other parents. Schools do not give out the phone numbers of other parents, by the way."

"We at the school pledge to continue teaching skills that will help secure a successful future for students. I will not be coming to your home to settle your problem, and some problems at school you need to let us handle; that is our responsibility, and it is what we are trained for. But please notify us to make us aware."

Riley then gave another example. "Monday morning can be very disturbing after a weekend. I remember a girlfriend and boyfriend who came into school, obviously in the middle of a fight. They had a bad weekend and brought it into school. The teacher notified us they couldn't teach with those two in the same class. My reaction? I let them go to the conference room for ten minutes to settle their problem, telling them that if they couldn't, they would both have a day off. I lucked out since they were both 18. Still, I notified their parents as they both left the building. The teacher and other students were then able to have a successful day. We will do the best we can for students, but we are here to teach, not babysit."

Another parent spoke up. "You suspended my kid, and according to your handbook, he got suspended for the number of days you FELT were appropriate. How can that be?"

"STOP right there," said Riley. "When I suspend a student, it is for as long as necessary. If the parent can settle the issue quickly, the student can come back the next day if they are ready to learn. We have that flexibility."

"Sometimes, rules are made to protect the building population. Having too many rules inhibits progress. If you don't respect your principal, that can become a problem. Trust that your child's principal is looking out for your child and the other students. Sometimes, a cooling-off period can be very important for a child—which is what a suspension essentially is. But cooling off for too long is not always a great idea. A long-term suspension also means the teacher needs to give makeup work. The student who is not in class does not learn as much."

Riley continued, "I remember being told by a principal at a conference about a student who waited while they tried to contact the parent about a classroom incident. The parent could not leave work, and the student was disruptive, cursing everyone out in the office. After a while, the school resource police officer was called to sit with the student, which meant the other 2000 students in the building did not have the police officer at needed places."

"Finally, the principal told the officer to take the student out of the building, either to her parent's worksite or to the police station. The police station was closer, so she was taken to a holding room there. The parent never got back to the principal until the afternoon. He finally came to the school after hours of not responding to calls. When he was told his daughter was at the police station, he went ballistic. Several people had to hold him back, and the resource officer was able to calm him down."

"When the superintendent found out, he was equally angry since the father was one of his golfing friends. He asked the school building principal why it had come down to that. 'You couldn't think of anything better?' The Principal replied, 'I just figured out a solution for the future. Next time, after the twelfth curse word and threat to my health or my staff's health, I can take her to your office to curse you and your secretary out.'"

The crowd didn't know whether to chuckle or gasp.

Riley continued, "Another principal told me his superintendent asked the staff to formulate a bully response. The result was based on the fact that we have been dealing with bullies forever. He said, 'The techniques and strategies we should use are the same we would use when dealing with our own children. Older siblings are usually pretty good at it. Now, when my staff locates a student who is being bullied, we assign athletes and coaches from girls' and boys' sports to act like big brothers and sisters.'"

"Remember, I am a poster child for the bullied. I use that as inspiration. I now have my picture around the school with the saying, 'I was bullied, and look where I am today.' I encourage our students to come talk to me if they feel threatened. There is no appointment necessary, and our talks remain confidential.'"

"You see, even though my parents were educators, I had to own the problem for myself. The fact is, I looked like I wanted to be bullied. And although we, as adults, must stand with students who are being bullied, like Mr. Alfred, my guardian angel, did for me, we must seek to empower them to become confident and own who they are and encourage them to seek secondary or vocational training or enter the military."

Another conference participant asked, "Why have we not been able to make school successful for all?"

Riley responded, "Our culture has changed drastically. Violent behavior and the availability to learn violence have become normalized. Today's parent must be a twenty-four parent. Two thoughts: If you really want to learn, you can. Everybody is talented, and everybody has a future. It is important to find out as early as possible what turns your child on. Then, encourage him to learn, grow, and seek a college degree. Looking for a job opening without preparing first is like opening the old phone books and looking for a miracle job. Make it happen through education! Don't just wait for it to happen."

Some final comments for the day from Riley: "I was asked about the twelve-month school year. Remember, summer is for warm weather, family outings, and a break in the learning process. Many students are fortunate enough to have parents who can send them to camp or on many different trips. Others spend their days playing games, watching movies, or playing sports. However, both scenarios should include reading reinforcement of past learning and preparing for new learning experiences. Of course, summer is hot, and year-round school would require the school system to budget for extra air conditioning in the summer months. That, combined with the importance of downtime, makes me shy away from 12-month schooling."

"I was also asked about homework overload. I do not like the word 'homework.' It should actually be called 'reinforcement of teaching' because that is the objective. Regardless, students should not be 'overloaded,' so parents need to be aware and supportive. Sorry, parents, you are definitely part of the learning equation."

"Here is how it should work. During the last five minutes of class, students are to be given a sheet to answer five questions from the day's work in class. If they answer them all correctly, they have no reinforcement work to take home and are given the next day's lesson in class. If they miss a question, they do get reinforcement work to take home and get help. The paper is signed by the parent and brought to school the next day. Two groups emerge, the one moving along and the one needing reinforcement. Everybody continues learning, and no one is overloaded."

The conference came to a close. Riley, the parents, teachers, and students all walked out a little more confident in the school system. And they all felt better equipped to work together to lead the next generation.

Chapter 40

Three Years Later

Riley's written dissertation on getting bullied in school became a very popular paper and was published in many educational journals. He became the third-generation Dr. Rossey. Even though he was looked upon with high prestige, he did not have any nameplates or door plates designating his doctorate status. He preferred "Riley" or "Rossey." With the school year nearing an end, the principal decided to retire, and everyone pushed for Riley to become the permanent principal.

With so many inside and outside candidates, Riley knew the competition and the politics would be interesting. One person who would not be rooting for Riley was good old Mr. Davis, who had been very quiet the last year. The high school principal makes more money than the middle school principal; this alone annoyed Mr. Davis. The question was, would it bother him enough to apply for the job? Most people thought not.

Although Mr. Davis claimed he would stay put because he loved the middle school, the fact was that he was not considered a great administrator, and the high school job would be more demanding. At the middle school, most everything ran either on automatic or was directed by the very capable assistants.

People weren't quiet about what they thought: "The real reason Davis doesn't want the job is that it's a lot more work than he's ever done. And now that Rossey has set a precedent of working a huge number of hours, Davis doesn't want to be bothered."

Still, Mr. Davis couldn't help but exude bad vibes about Rossey. "What a disgrace to the district it would be to appoint him." "If Rossey gets this job, the district will really go downhill." "The males will have no respect for him." And,

"Of course, since Rossey has been working, he works fifteen hours a day. He won't last long. He's making more work with less pay."

Mr. Davis failed to recognize the obvious: the staff thought very highly of Riley. In fact, he was one of the favorites, and most of the staff was pulling for him.

Chapter 41

Interviewing for the Principal Job

I n answering questions for the position of the high school principal, Riley always stressed that students were his priority. And his track record proved this.

When Riley was asked questions about working with Mr. Davis, his answer was straightforward. "I do not expect any problems whatsoever." When pressed further, he responded, "I have more than conquered my action with bullies and could not be more focused on making sure that whatever comes up, I can handle. You've read the reports of how I was bullied in school by many, including Mr. Davis and his family, who continually came against the Rosseys, inflicting fear. In the worst English, I can say, 'His tactics ain't gonna work.' Something like he has never seen will make him hide quickly." That ended those questions.

Regarding his vision for the school, Riley stated, "I'm in the hot seat every day. It keeps me fresh. My priorities include hiring the best teachers to serve our students and empowering paraprofessionals to be student-oriented. I've developed and implemented award-winning curriculums in math related to sports, computers, medicine, crime-fighting, exercise, and eating properly."

Riley always worked to move ahead in the future of math but would never leave the students behind. He tied certain popular subjects to math, and it worked. The math scores for the high school had soared. "I allowed teachers time to develop their own curriculum in their fields of expertise and research those of other school systems as well. Teachers I have mentored have grown by attending various workshops, encouraging them to create new ideas as well as copy other districts' successes."

After two days of interviews, no one could come close to Dr. Rossey. He scored a perfect score. Even a close friend of Mr. Davis on the committee could not even think of why the district should not hire Riley.

The next Board of Education meeting was packed with teachers, parents, students, former students, Dr. Rossey's family, Mr. Alfred's entire staff, and many other supporters of Riley. When the announcement was made recommending Riley to be the new high school principal, the audience erupted in cheers. The Board President had to settle the audience down.

When it came time to vote, the Board voted unanimously. Dean Brenner said, "Now you may clap for our new high school principal, Dr. Riley Rossey." The audience cheered, and Riley began the hugging. Then Mr. Brenner said, "We'll take a fifteen-minute break. I think it's appropriate." And a roar went up again.

As Riley began his tenure as principal, the local press asked a big question: Is school for everyone? Riley weighed in, "That's a good question. College is not for everyone. Military is not for everyone. Trades are not for everyone. There are many hints as to what a student is thinking when he cuts classes, has high absenteeism, becomes a discipline problem, sleeps or daydreams in class, or focuses on his problems at home. We need to find out the why and take action. Because, yes, high school IS for everyone."

As promised, Riley made sure he had a good staff. One of the student counselors was a student favorite. He was who the kids would flock to when there was a problem and was involved with students in after-school and weekend activities. Whether it was a female issue, a male issue, or a home problem that affected attendance at school, Mr. Z was there. Riley donned him the "counselor deluxe."

Mr. Z was not judgmental, which the students loved. He always gave them time to think of solutions. He did not take the students out of class but instead would meet them during lunch or other times they were available. He was all ears.

The teachers also loved Mr. Z. Counselors were prohibited from evaluating teachers or talking about their teaching in the school environment, which ensured a team approach. But Mr. Z actively supported the teachers, recognizing they were going the extra mile.

Parents loved him, too, as he very honestly addressed their concerns about life after high school.

Mr. Z's caseload multiplied each day as the word got around that he could be trusted. Riley teased, "I just don't know if we can afford all the message pads we need for all the students, parents, and teachers who seek Mr. Z."

Chapter 42

SUMMER REQUIREMENTS

The teachers and administrators battled it out as Dr. Rossey required the teachers to take at least one course or workshop during the summer. He said the course should include updated information on the subject matter the teacher specialized in.

"What about being paid and making it an option instead of a requirement?" griped one teacher. "I have worked for the past ten years as a history teacher. Do I need to go back in history to be a better teacher?"

Riley was adamant in making sure the teachers were updating their skills. To ensure compliance, he added a section regarding "course improvement" to their yearly evaluation.

Of course, Mr. Davis didn't implement this new plan, saying, "Here goes the Rossey screw-up again." Davis told his teachers, "Don't worry. I already spoke to the superintendent. She is against the requirement and against having teachers work without pay."

Chapter 43

Other Issues for the School and Dr. Rossey

Sometimes, being the high school principal was an uphill battle.

Dr. Rossey was amazed when he found out how many students live full-time with their grandparents, and he wanted to start a training program with the grandparents after school. However, this was knocked down by the Board of Education. They even recommended against having conference calls or emailing information to help support these individuals despite Dr. Rossey identifying 15 such grandparents who would benefit. It did not make a difference.

Even when several teachers agreed to help establish this program after school, the answer was still no. The Board feared it would set a bad precedent and would eventually require more cost to the school system. Instead, they advised to offer the training at parent-teacher association meetings.

Another issue Riley had to face was students who were up to no good in the bathrooms. One of the assistant principals decided the best way to handle that situation was to lock the bathrooms during the day and give a key to several teachers who would be monitoring the hallway. Many thought this was too involved, to which the assistant principal replied, "If we just allow students to go and come as they want, we are making them miss valuable time in class."

When one parent brought in a doctor's note saying her son needed to have a key because of medical issues, Dr. Rossey had no choice but to give in. Then he found out that not only was the student smoking in the bathroom, but according to two snitches, he also urinated on the floor to get back at the administration.

When Dr. Rossey met with the student's parent, he was pretty straightforward. "This is a training field. If your child is unable to abide by rules, how long do you think he will last in a job?"

Then there was the day Dr. Rossey walked into the gym and saw twenty students sitting in the bleachers. He asked why, and the teachers responded that these students were unprepared and got a zero for the day. Meanwhile, they were on their cell phones, laughing, and not in a safe place as the teacher was supervising the students who were prepared.

"Why were they not given written assignments that would take longer than a period to complete? And why are they not sitting in the vicinity of the teacher so they can be supervised?" Riley questioned.

At a special education meeting, a parent challenged Riley with a question. She asked what specific goals her child's individualized program was targeting. She claimed that the paperwork she received was generic and only had the teacher's signature, with no outline plan or next steps.

Riley called the parent in after speaking to his team. "I was told you did not sign the document for your child's individualized program. That is perfectly understandable since the team could not answer some of the questions to your level of understanding. I would like to schedule a meeting with you and the teachers. It is to everyone's advantage to make this a real document and not just follow the law."

Chapter 44

DR. ROSSEY GETS IN TROUBLE FOR TELLING THE TRUTH

D r. Rossey never shied away from telling the truth, even when others didn't want to hear it. Sometimes, it got him in trouble.

One day, Dr. Rossey made waves by baring his soul to the press. It started innocently when a news reporter asked for his response to someone who stated that schools were political. "So is the rest of the world," said Riley. And then he explained. By the time the superintendent got wind of all he said, Dr. Rossey had been questioned by all the Board members and people with special privileges.

"He is not speaking for this district and should not be listened to," said the superintendent, who was beside herself.

The main point stated in the article was that the schools needed to leave the hiring and firing to the Board of Education and that people getting favorable con-tracts must follow the bidding procedure for all the departments. Riley summed up his stance, "We need to stop allowing parents of the more influential students to get what they want while other parents are left outside the loop."

Then he brought up how he had proposed to help grandparents who were raising their grandchildren but was halted. "What a great resource it would be for the grandparents and the school system. We have already identified grandparents in our district who could use support. But we also discovered that many of these grandparents are very educated people who are willing to work as mentors, teacher assistants, or just help out in the lunchroom and hallways."

During an administrative meeting, Riley was asked to respond to security issues. "The question is how can we cover thirty doors in a building that holds over two thousand students? And how can we know who is outside the gates waiting for us to let our guard down? The superintendent did not want to include additional training time for such an endeavor, as that would have cost more than is allotted in the present budget."

Yet another concern came directly from the staff. "We have parents who want daily progress on their student."

This request seemed impossible as many teachers had over one hundred students and could not report on them every day. Riley again suggested, "Test whether or not the students understood the lesson with four or five simple questions at the end of each class. How they respond becomes the report. Those who did not understand the lesson can take home the sheet and have their parent work with them."

School monitoring was also an often brought up subject. "Cameras in the schools are an old idea; now there is more sophisticated and expensive equipment. But you cannot have a camera to watch for intruders at every door. And the bathrooms and gym lockers are off-limits for obvious reasons. So teachers have a responsibility to watch out for suspicious characters."

Knowing the responsibilities already heaped on the teachers, Riley replied, "I'm not a big believer in using teachers as monitors or burdening them with the responsibility of overseeing sophisticated equipment. But I do believe in rewarding students who have done a good job of notifying staff of such problems. Snitches have a special place in my heart, and they can count on me to help them out of jams. Also, student council members can use their rewards from such services to fund their end-of-the-year functions."

Concerning the hot topic of suspensions, Riley stated, "It's widely known that I do not like the concept of having a set number of days for suspensions. So, how can we maintain consistency? Easy, welcome to the world of being in charge and having a grievance system. Let's consider what other administrators say. For one, we have mandatory laws in this country that are not always consistent. Second, we must keep in mind that the goal of a suspension is to encourage the individual to change their behavior."

"So when a parent complained about me suspending a student for throwing a dangerous object at a school bus and asked, 'What do you want me to do with him for two days?' I gave an arrogant answer, 'Let him throw things at the windows of your house and see how you feel.'"

That did not go over well with the superintendent.

Riley was a stickler for the proper use of cell phones in school. "If I thought students could keep their cell phones in their pockets and never take them out, I might agree with allowing kids to have them. But it doesn't work that way in school. I have observed students talking on their phones in the hallway and playing games on their phones under the desk during a lecture. But safety is paramount. And the importance of having a cell phone goes back to safety. When there is an intruder in the school, neither students nor staff should be far away from a phone."

"Our lockdown plan is reviewed weekly and is posted in every room in the school. It includes the policy on cell phones. Our paraprofessionals have been trained extensively and know to keep their phones active and be fully aware of the emergency directory available in every classroom."

"So, what happens when we take a phone away from a child who does not follow the rules? We make the parent come to the school to pick it up. Why? Because the parent will be angry enough that losing the phone is not worth it. Unless there is a specific medical reason why the parent cannot come in, we keep the phone until they appear. Keep in mind, this rule was discussed with parents many times, so it should be no surprise."

The cafeteria seemed to be a breeding ground for issues in the school, but this was nothing new. Riley made the case, "I remember getting bullied in the cafeteria almost more than in any other place. There just seems to be more opportunity because of all the noise, pushing, and shoving, particularly in the food line. The teachers on duty work hard to try to keep the peace."

"We have kids under the federal lunch program, and we must ensure they are provided for. Now, sometimes the food is not to their liking—there are specific meals the students identify as 'mystery meat'—but as long as we follow food service guidelines, we are doing the best we can."

"Regardless, kids would generally rather have chips, ice cream, and other sugary items, which causes the problem of students sneaking into the teachers' rooms and getting sugar drinks. I like to think the teachers are watching. And when they do that, the kids' money actually goes to the teacher's group machine. Who gets the profits from that, I wonder?"

Chapter 45

Making Strides

Overall, Dr. Rossey's practices had quite positive effects. For one thing, students and teachers began working together to plan great philanthropic events. Riley was particularly proud of the success of the blood drive. At first, it didn't work because the kids did not want the ordinary incentives offered. Then, one of the students came to Dr. Rossey and said, "I have an idea."

"Go ahead, I'm listening."

"During the last blood drive, many of the students were taken out of classes they liked the most. Why not let them choose what class to miss? They may want to coordinate with their friends and participate together. Also, offer free movie tickets, soda, and popcorn for motivation."

Every blood drive after, they had to have an additional Red Bus come because so many kids wanted to give blood. Riley learned that sometimes, you need to break the mold and change your thinking process, just like he taught the students.

Students also became involved in helping schedule speakers. The staff learned, through trial and error, that a speaker liked by a group of adults won't necessarily enthrall students. Without input from the students, even a so-called dynamic speaker was doomed for failure. The students helped the staff look for speakers with particular criteria, such as those who dressed cool, had good lines, were humorous, and involved the students in interesting activities. All those things led to overwhelming cooperation and interest.

Not everything went smoothly. Riley often had to address parents who had a problem with a teacher and called a board member instead of calling the teacher's supervisor, assistant principal, or superintendent. This just annoyed everyone and put the staff on guard, causing them to avoid the kid and his problems. Each time he spoke publicly, Riley reminded the parents, "Please, follow the chain of command so we can best help your child. If you are more interested in bashing a teacher than trying to help solve a problem, perhaps it is time to take a break from all that is pulling you away from your child and talk to and guide your kid. That is your top priority. Parenting is a 24/7 job, whether you agree or not."

"Spend quality time with your children every day, not just on holidays or special occasions. Sometimes, you have to ask your children questions they don't want to answer. But when you do, deep inside, they will know you care."

Regarding the topic of parenting, there was much Riley wanted to convey, and he wasn't shy about sharing. "It's never too early to put ideas in kids' heads about what they can do after they finish school. Expose them to various careers. Point them toward a career that fits their interests."

"Don't overlook vocational technical training. There are many vocational opportunities available, both part-time and full-time jobs. Don't worry so much about your child's IQ or test scores. Every kid is gifted in some way. Find out what they want to do. I'm not just talking about kids who say they want to be a football player, actor, or singer. Then, seek others in that field and ask how they got started. It takes hard work and dedication to help guide your kids. Use creativity, like teaching the kid who loves basketball but was never good enough to play that he might be a good coach."

"Being bullied is not uncommon, but it doesn't have to define a person's life. My story of bullying ended because I took control. One of the most important parts of the solution was that my parents got involved but didn't take over. They shut down my computer and made sure the second I mentioned the word bully, they went to the right people to stop it immediately, always including me in the process."

"So now let's go back to the teachers. Find out the best way to communicate with your child's teachers. Be realistic. Some teachers have many students throughout the day. Yes, they are being paid and are fortunate to have a job that lasts only ten months and allows them to leave work early each day, but there is much you don't see. They have families and a life of their own, just like you. They have to go for retraining constantly and prepare lessons daily. And they work many extra hours, often late into the evening."

"Set some boundaries. Popping in on teachers without notice is not only a no-no but also very rude. If you want to observe the teacher with your child, go through the high school administrators to get permission. Their job requires them to oversee the classroom. We strive to help teachers do the right things every day."

"Supervisors do have the permission to pop into the classroom at different times; they can ensure that the teacher is doing his or her job. As an administrator, I think that's fair. Sometimes, what they find is not up to par, but everyone has a bad hair day. A good supervisor will recognize this and return on a different day. The evaluation is about constructive criticism. It's not that hard to find out who the good teachers are—the kids know, and so does the staff. And former students are also especially keen on that."

"Teachers are important. I think every student who goes to any kind of school will tell you there has been at least one teacher in their life who had a positive influence on them. Maybe it was something they said or something that they taught. Ask successful adults."

"So, if the teacher's job is to teach, what is the parent's job? For one, it is to spend time with your child. How much is enough? The most you can and more if necessary. Make sure your children have resources to make them better students. Cut some of the frills out of your life and hang out with your kids, getting them the help they need. Projects around the house can wait. Ten years from now, they won't matter. But your child's progress will. Childhood does not last forever."

"School structure is not for everyone, but the need for knowledge is. Some students might think algebra and geometry are irrelevant, but they will use those skills in their own way. Students learn how to learn, sometimes in an environment that stretches them, and then they wind up in colleges, vocational programs, or managing or owning small businesses. Our job is to prepare them so they can live a full, happy, and self-sustaining life."

"At our school, we have guidance counselors and nurses I am very fond of. Sometimes, the nurses are more in touch with the kids than counselors. I've seen guidance counselors who make appointments and then play find-the-counselor. Counselors need to find the kids. And I worry when I see guidance counselors spend more time in their offices than in and around the classroom, actually seeing what is going on. However, a counselor can be instrumental in shaping a student. They often give some real concrete information on what a student can do to get into college. Every kid matures at a different time in their life. Many students return after graduation and tell us they would not have been successful were it not for their teachers and counselors."

"I'm proud of the people I work with, I'm proud of our parents, and, most of all, I'm proud of our students. We are all growing together."

Chapter 46

Ending the Year on a Tough Note

That year full of ups and downs was nearly over. But there was more to come.

One morning as the students were entering the building, one of the school's toilets was blown up. After hours of questioning students and staff who had been in the area, a suspect was identified. Among other incriminating evidence, three trustworthy students agreed that the student was guilty. One of the most valuable tools for a principal is to have some snitches in the building.

The student in question denied any wrongdoing. Still, his father was called in. He arrived screaming and threatening all kinds of actions against the school.

In situations like this, usually, the perpetrator is someone who is not worried about repercussions. This time was no different. However, the stress of the entire situation eventually caused the student to admit his wrongdoing. The most upset person was the dad, who couldn't apologize enough. It was fortunate nobody got hurt. Knowing he could not trust the student again, Dr. Rossey arranged homebound instruction with a strong counseling component for the remainder of the year. The student was warned he had no wiggle room.

The cost of the damage was three hundred dollars. Money is always part of the equation. Dealing with the school budget was something Riley often had to think about. It was even more difficult to consider at the end of the year.

With just four weeks left in the year, a parent came to school wanting her child taken out of a teacher's class. The first words from Riley's mouth were, "Did you speak to the teacher?"

"I can't stand her. My son says she is mean, and all the kids hate her."

Riley responded that there were a few weeks left in the school year, and moving him would cause a ripple of issues with his schedule. The woman left irate.

The following day, Riley got a call from the superintendent asking why the student had not been moved to another class. With his hands tied, Riley was forced to make the change, later discovering that the parent was shopping buddies with the superintendent.

Then, a complaint was made that a special education student was being bullied by another student. So, what did the counselor do? He moved the bullied student to four new classes, while the bully himself was left alone. Where was the counselor's head? It seems it was easier to move the special education student than the student who was getting As in the classes. What a poor response. But that wasn't the final bullying complaint of the year.

One of Riley's responsibilities was to attend special education conferences, where the staff would review an individual student's plan and progress. When he attended the conference for Jimmy Bitolli, things exploded. Within the first ten minutes, Jimmy's parents, who were legally separated, began screaming at each other while Jimmy sat there mortified. Jimmy apologized for his parents after the conference. Imagine that—two adults acting like kids and the kid responding like an adult!

After his parents got themselves under control, Jimmy said that his teacher, Mr. Hankins, was constantly bullying him, and he didn't know what to do. Riley's face got red with anger. He immediately checked with other students in Mr. Hankins' class and found out they were also being treated unfairly. Then, lo and behold, Riley discovered that Mr. Hankins was best friends with Mr. Davis, which explained a lot.

Riley consulted with his dad. Richard Rossey advised, "Get a written statement from the students and then make sure you observe Mr. Hankins on a daily basis for at least two weeks. By that time, he will come to you wondering what is going on. Then, have a conference with Mr. Hankins, laying out everything you have learned. And make sure you put it all in writing."

Summer finally arrived. What a year!

Chapter 47

BEYOND THE CLASSROOM

On a Saturday morning, Riley went outside to have a cup of coffee in his backyard and rehash some other moments in his career. One of those moments was when Mrs. Jones came into Riley's office in distress because her daughter Mary was doing well in school and her son Henry was not. Both children had the same parents, were raised with love and attention, and had been good babies. But all the teachers complained about Henry.

Having heard this many times from parents, Riley offered his version of why two children from the same home can be so different.

"Here is how it works. Mrs. Jones. When God decided to bless you with your second child, He reviewed your progress. He found out Mary never gave anyone a hard time and that you and your husband had actually raved about her. So He decided to give you Henry. God has His reasons," said Riley. "That is the way it works. That is why you got Henry."

Mrs. Jones and Riley laughed hard, and Mrs. Jones, who respected Riley, thanked him for his calming effect. "Believe me. With the love and respect in your household, God will bless you and your children."

Riley also remembered the student who almost caused a huge disruption at one of the graduation ceremonies. This was one of the few students Riley could honestly say he was happy to see leave. Eddie was more than just a prankster. He was a dangerous, daring kid—both at school and while driving on the road.

It seemed like Eddie was going to go out with a bang. He was given many breaks at school by the teachers and the school administrators. Well, at graduation, Riley put one of the assistant principals backstage to ensure none of the kids would do anything stupid.

That's how Mike Creece saw Eddie preparing to light a firecracker. Mr. Creece reacted quickly; off the stage went Eddie as the surprised graduates looked on. The guest speaker kept speaking, and the crowd clapped, appreciating the prevention of what could have been a major concern.

Eddie was pulled off the stage while he cursed at Mr. Creece. Then, with a match and a firecracker still in his hand, he yelled, "I wasn't going to light it! I was just playing!"

As the ceremony concluded, Eddie's family came forward, screaming about Eddie not marching with his class. Even after Riley calmly spoke to them, they were still fuming mad. The superintendent backed Riley and told the parents that the school was considering pressing charges. Two weeks later, Eddie got his diploma in the mail, and the family left town quickly.

And there were good memories. Riley remembered a student who never missed a single day of school, from nursery school through high school. He certainly got a special award and a great speech from Riley. David Decicci received a personal check and congratulatory card from Riley. It was a great tribute to a great family.

Riley sure influenced many. And his influence was felt. Once, Riley received a phone call from a nearby school asking why he did not recommend a former student for a teaching job. Their question revolved around the fact that she had gotten straight As during her college education. Riley remembered her well.

"I would not recommend her for a high school or middle school position. You know, when I had her in my class, she was very bright and articulate. But when she answered questions from the interview panel, we all had the same feeling: the kids would chase her out of class. She should apply for an elementary or preschool job."

"Sometimes, we can't get past the stage of not showing confidence in a student who has graduated from our school. In her case, I could not see it. Even if I had her substitute teacher and had people keep an eye on her, I felt the learning curve was way too long. This was especially true with the number of streetwise kids she would be dealing with."

Chapter 48

Why Some Students Don't Make It

D r. Richard Rossey was very quick-witted. He told Riley many stories that caused him to think. One of his famous stories he often told at conferences and to parents was, Who's really to blame?

The story begins with a parent and her son discussing three employers who had fired him. The mom, who did nothing but help promote her son, was baffled when he lost his third job at just twenty-three years old.

The son, Undley, approached his last boss to discuss why he had been unsuccessful. The boss said, "It was probably the college you attended. They did not teach you what the real world is all about. Your evaluations came back average to below average. You had plenty of time to change. You constantly asked the wrong questions and were expecting answers that would help with your excuses. I cannot tolerate average employees. I recommend you go back to your college professors and ask their take on you."

So Undley decided his former boss was not the kind of person he should have worked for. His college counselor and some of his professors answered the same question: Why was Undley not successful?

"I remember specifically, as your counselor said, Mr. Stevens. I told you what to do, and you would not listen. As a matter of fact, you put most of the blame on your professors. Your name always came up as the head of all the social events. Never did you receive any special academic awards. And I remember that both your mom and I begged you to change your behavior. Your answer was always the same. 'I'm busting my butt. What do you want me to do differently?'"

The college professor said, "Go talk to your high school counselors. Maybe they were the ones who misdirected you."

Undley went to his high school counselor, who immediately recognized him. The counselor asked, "Do you have family here? What is going on with you?"

Undley explained that he was fired from three jobs, and no one could give him a good answer for why he kept failing.

"Well," said the counselor, "We all remember you very well. We tried helping your mom change your attitude, but you kept blaming everyone else for why you were not getting the grades you thought you deserved. Your records showed numerous tardy and discipline problems. Your test scores were well below normal. I think if you go back to your junior high staff, you may find better answers as to why you are having so many problems holding a job. And by the way, you promised the military recruiters to speak with them. I lined you up to contact them, which you never did."

Undley returned to the junior high school counselor, who said, "Look, we still remember you spent more time blaming teachers for poor grades and having your mom harass us all, which was brought on because of you. It would be a good idea for you to go to the elementary school and talk to them."

When he walked into the elementary school, several veteran teachers were startled, thinking he had children in the district. One of the teachers said, "Maybe he's looking for a custodial job or looking to wash dishes in the lunchroom." After looking at some past records, he continued to be baffled as to why he was hearing such negative feedback.

As a last resort, Undley headed over to his pre-school. Everyone there was so nice and said what a wonderful child he was and how much he was liked. That made him happy until the owner came out and reminded him that his mother was forced to pull him out because he was so disruptive.

As he headed home, his mom asked, "How were your visits?"

His first comment was, "I would have done a whole lot better if you and Dad had stayed together."

His mom defended herself, "Your younger siblings are all doing fine. As a matter of fact, your brother Willie wrote a paper saying that thanks to you being such a jerk, he learned to go in the opposite direction and be the best he can."

"Yes," she continued, "I'm a single parent who worked three jobs and stayed on your case about school. I had to take unpaid time to go to school and have parent conferences with the teachers and principals. I think your next visit should be to the church we attend. Reverend Slipdiss will be able to place the blame where it should be."

Upon their discussion, Reverend Slipdiss said, "Come into my office, Undley." After a long discussion, the reverend said, "I'll be right back." He returned holding a very big mirror and said to Undley, "Here is the blame you've been seeking. This is the only person to blame." Undley looked into the giant-size mirror. "You came here seeking an answer. You attended school without a purpose and are now living without a purpose. Without a purpose, you will fail. Return to church, and we will help you find your purpose."

Chapter 49

Not a Happy Birthday for a Teacher

Other significant memories came to mind as Riley reminisced. One involved Mr. Pete Fraptor, the diesel mechanic teacher who had a birthday recognized by one of his students.

Jack brought in brownies exclusively for Mr. Pete. Mr. Pete was grateful and looked forward to having the brownies with a cup of coffee after class. He went to the teacher's room to eat the brownies and left one in the refrigerator for later. They were really big and tasted great.

As he began his afternoon class, Pete suddenly felt dizzy and had to sit down. When he tried to get up, he stumbled. Several students steadied him. They called the office, and Dr. Rossey came running with the school nurse. Henrietta said, "Call 911!" Riley followed the ambulance to the hospital in his car.

When they got to the hospital, Pete was put in a holding room in the emergency area awaiting examination. Meanwhile, announcements came across the speakers in the hospital like crazy, paging doctors and nurses to the emergency room.

Pete called for Riley, "Hey man, I must be dreaming. There are people coming in here full of blood." That is when Riley looked at Pete's bloodshot eyes and knew this had all the makings of a teacher on drugs. When Riley asked him if he took any prescription drugs, Pete said, "I don't even take aspirin. But I did have an amazing brownie. I left one in the refrigerator in the teacher's lounge if you want it. I don't think I'll be going back anytime soon."

Riley quickly called his assistant to go and get the brownie and take the nurse with him. Riley was not surprised that when the police checked it out, they discovered it was a hash brownie.

Jack was brought into the assistant principal's office, where the police and his parents were waiting. Jack admitted to loading the brownie. His father had to be held back from grabbing Jack by the neck. Then, the real panic was when Jack's father said, "Jack knows Pete and I are friends. We fish, hunt, and watch sports together."

Riley returned from the hospital while the group was meeting. It was up to Riley to hand out the punishment. It was not what Jack or his parents wanted to hear. Jack was suspended for the remainder of the school year, sixteen days. He was placed on home instruction and was to take his finals at home. He was barred from graduation and all graduation activities. He was barred from being anywhere on campus for the rest of the school year and would not be able to pick up his diploma until the school year was over. A police report was filed. There were no happy campers in that family. Riley's quick response was received with approval from the staff and the students.

Another incident Riley reminded himself of was with a student named Paul Hughes. Paul was a senior and one of the best students in the senior class. One day, Paul was very arrogant to everyone he came in contact with, speaking in curses and threats. One instructor told Riley, "The kid is off the wall."

When Riley went to get Paul, Paul cursed him out. Riley called the school police, who met with Paul in Riley's office. Riley asked Paul what was going on.

Paul said, "Okay, Dr. R, why did you call me down here?"

"You need to be seen by the nurse for possibly being under the influence of a controlled, dangerous substance," said Riley.

"Who the heck told you that?"

"Paul, cool it. I've only seen you for five minutes. I'm losing patience. So watch the way you talk to me."

Just then, a police officer and Paul's mom walked into the office. Paul said, "I want my lawyer before I say another word, especially with Robo Cop here."

That did it. The officer took Paul outside the office, "We can make this real easy or real hard. What's your choice?" the officer said.

Paul went back into Riley's office. As he did, he kicked the door so hard he put a hole in it. At that point, the officer took out his handcuffs, and his mom began to cry. Riley intervened, "You can keep your mouth shut and go home with your mom, or I can let the police take over. What's your choice?"

The mom was very upset. She felt there was no due process and that Riley was very nasty. Meanwhile, the nurse who examined Paul said what Riley expected: the student was on some drug.

Riley suspended Paul until a report on the drug test could be confirmed and told him that he would have to pay for the door. His mom said, "I'm a single parent, and I don't have spare money."

Riley replied, "Your son is making good money in the work release program. This is his bill, not yours. Let him pay."

But Paul's mom took it up with the superintendent, who rescinded the student's suspension and said, "The school will pay for the door."

Riley was furious. But his superior had the final say.

Riley always prided himself on doing his job properly. But sometimes, parents stick up for their kids at the wrong time. And so do school officials.

Chapter 50

RILEY'S OFFICE POSTERS

It was important to Riley that when someone walked into his conference room, they would see inspirational posters. Many he had hanging were created by students; others were created by Riley himself. Some of his favorites over the years were:

- *The most important job of a parent is their child's success and health. Be positive.*

- *Be nice to a kid who may look like a pushover. You may be working for someone like him one day.*

- *Be nice and respect your elders. If you don't have a good word, keep your thoughts private.*

- *Working in what you call a menial job for menial pay is a start, not a finish.*

- *If you don't learn to discipline yourself, others may discipline you in a way you won't like.*

- *Think, talk, and then act. Be a great mind, then innovate.*

- *The hardest worker doesn't always win. But working hard instills good habits.*

- *Learn from your mistakes, and don't repeat them. If you make the same mistake twice, stop and think. Then start again.*

- *Press past distractions. Keep the vision in front of you.*

- *Keep your purpose at the top of your list.*

- *When you aren't doing well, hit the reset button.*

- *Sometimes rejection is protection.*

- *If it were easy, everyone would do it.*

- *Mean what you say; say what you mean.*

- *Failure is never final unless you want it to be.*

- *Who you follow will decide your future. Make a smart choice.*

- *When you stop the fear, start the engine again.*

- *Consistency of effort and follow-up are crucial.*

- *Make modifications and adjustments when you must.*

There were so many other thoughts that Riley remembered.

One time, Riley went to the student parking lot following graduation. Students had kegs of beer in their trucks and cars. Riley was adamant about not having one student drink in the parking lot. When he called the parents, some actually said, "Don't worry, he'll only have one beer." When the police came, the kids got the message. The police took it all. Protecting students and school liability were two musts.

As Riley's mind wandered, he remembered another past incident. Jimmy decided to throw an object, which hit a window and broke it. His father apologized to Riley, made his son pay for the window, and took away his car keys for the weekend. Jimmy apologized, accepted his punishment, and never got in that kind of trouble again.

Riley remembered a student who had no discipline problems in school and explained why. "My grandma had a broom, my grandpa's belt, and my dad's shoe. She said if she got any bad news from school or my parents, I could choose which one I wanted her to use. Just the look from my 80-year-old grandma was enough to keep me out of trouble."

Riley understood that the student's respect did not come from a beating, which actually never occurred. It came from discipline, although many now consider actual discipline child abuse. Ask other adults, and you'll find many learned to do the right thing out of respect for their adult figures.

Something that had bothered Riley through the years was the use of bad language, although he understood that, sometimes, we are all guilty of using bad language. Still, when the coach of an athletic team constantly spoke with colorful words, Riley had to call him on it. He reminded the coaches, "We are not here to embarrass or curse out our students. If you do by accident, don't be afraid to apologize."

That thought reminded Riley of a famous football coach's conversation with a college professor. The professor had a doctorate in education and prepared students for medical careers. The professor said to the coach, "Look, I earn a good sum of money for educating students, but you earn fifty times more than I do. There's something wrong with that system. I studied hard and worked my tail off."

The coach's verbal comeback was simple, "I put eighty thousand people in the football stadium and work with sponsors that sell more than 'Professor Jones' t-shirts. People spend tons of money at football games, which goes to the school."

Riley felt and taught that being late to or absent from school directly related to how the individual would act later in life. Any blatant disregard for responsibility was habit-forming. Riley's always tried to instill in students that being early is being on time, and to arrive on time is to arrive late.

Riley remembered a teacher who received twelve sick days a year according to her contract. At the end of twenty-five years, she had used every single sick day.

She was a believer in mental health days, but Riley couldn't help but think about how much instruction her students lost.

Chapter 51

RETIREMENT – AFTER THIRTY YEARS

As Riley celebrated thirty years of educational service, he decided it was time to leave his career. He had never married. Although he had met eligible women along the way, he never dated them. It could be said that he had been married to his job. And unbelievably, James Davis and Riley Rossey existed in the same system. Many credit Riley, who ducked punch after punch, making James look either silly or stupid.

James Davis's lack of knowledge was his relationship while "shooting information from the hip." Riley included everyone in his decision-making for the students and the school. Riley was described as the picture-perfect principal, while James was busy trying to figure who could do his work, always calling it training people for his job. "Yeah, right!" was the answer from his staff.

At Riley's retirement dinner, the staff gave him a great sendoff. At all the tables, they had lunchboxes with Riley's name to symbolize the days he overcame being bullied in the cafeteria. They all wore hats that said, "What's up, Doc?" as a nod to his doctorate. Then, the biggest tearjerker for Riley was a picture with a group of graduates and present-day students holding a sign that said, "Without you, we would not have made it."

The speeches were endless—so many wanted to give their thanks. But the most important and impactful moment was when Mr. Alfred came to the podium and told Riley, "I just want to tell you, you were not like your dad, but I enjoyed every moment." The crowd couldn't stop clapping, and the now older but still spry man couldn't stop crying. They hugged each other, and Mr. Alfred whispered in Riley's ear. "Your Mr. Davis will regret the day that he ever bullied you. I guarantee you that." Somehow, Riley knew that the strange episodes from Mr. Alfred were a gift.

However, Mr. Davis, who refused to retire despite his advancing age, became the new high school principal, easily winning approval because of his connections.

Chapter 52

A New Turn

Two years into his retirement, Riley was feeling tired after spending the day writing and reading, and went to bed not feeling quite right. He was startled by the ringing of his doorbell at midnight. He went to the door, but no one seemed to be there. He looked through the peephole, "Who is there?" There was no answer.

Riley thought maybe the bell had a short, or maybe he had dreamed the whole thing. Just when he was ready to go back to sleep, a man in a blue suit appeared before him in his house, scaring the daylights out of Riley.

"What do you want? And how did you get in?"

"Don't fear me. Just relax and listen. My name is Mr. Helper, and I am from Principal Heaven."

"What?" said Riley.

"I'm here representing the Principal Heaven Group. My name is Mr. Life Helper, and I am the leader for those who have completed a successful life as high school administrators."

At first, Riley believed he was dreaming. But Mr. Helper convinced him that what he was experiencing was real. Dr. Riley Rossey had entered a new realm of existence.

Mr. Helper asked Riley to come with him to meet some of the other administrators. Riley began to wonder and slapped himself in the face. "Does this mean I will get to see my grandfather and my dad?"

Riley followed Mr. Helper outside, where there was a special car. Riley's neighbor was bringing his trash can out for morning pickup.

"Hi, Mr. Verde," Riley said to his neighbor, who saw and heard nothing. Mr. Verde always acknowledged Riley.

The next thing he knew, Riley was in Mr. Helper's car. The car had some strange controls, and as Mr. Helper moved forward very quickly, Riley asked, "Where is the smoke coming from?"

Mr. Helper answered, "That is not smoke. It is clouds. We are entering our destination."

When the car stopped, they were in front of a house that resembled a luxury hotel. "Come on, get out of the car, and I'll show you around," said Mr. Helper.

Chapter 53

Visiting Principal Heaven

When all the clouds finally cleared, Riley recognized the old neighborhood where he grew up.

Mr. Helper again encouraged Riley to get out of the car and follow him, saying, "We have an issue and an opportunity, and we need your assistance. Principal Davis has fallen ill and has been taken to the hospital. That's the issue. The opportunity is that your old high school, under his care, is quickly going downhill. Let me show you."

Suddenly, Riley was given a look into what the future held for his old school if Mr. Davis's reign as principal were to continue. Riley gasped at what he saw, recognizing that in just the next two years, parents and students would have a bigger say in the school, and not a good one at that.

Principal James Davis will hire new teachers. That alone is a telling factor. Thanks to Mr. Davis, the Board of Education, and the superintendent, the district will be micromanaged by parents and students, which will be great for Davis because he will blame them when there are complaints.

The district's enrollment will quickly drop as parents send their children to private schools or begin homeschooling them. Instead of helping students with problems, Mr. Davis will manage to kick them out of school. And because the school name irks Mr. Davis, he will make sure it is changed from Dr. Riley Rossey High School.

As Riley continued to peer into the future, he noticed that from the outside, the school looked neglected. In the vision, Riley saw Mr. Alfred walking by crying, no doubt at the condition of the school he had so lovingly maintained.

Not only did the school look terrible, but the teachers and even the police had become tired of the school's neglect. There were numerous reports of speeding cars and students hanging in the parking lot. There were drug busts and fights before and after school, and little attention was given to solutions.

Mr. Helper had more news for Riley. "James Davis will finally be recognized as the con man everyone has known since day one of his educational career. After being reamed out privately by the Board of Education, he will be under pressure from students, parents, teachers, and state department officials. He will begin taking medication—some prescribed by his doctor and some not. He will lose sleep and will not be recognizable at work. The school administration will decide to micromanage even more."

"Students and staff will not know who is in charge. The assistant principals will try to help, but Mr. Davis will continue his attitude of being a one-man show. All the loyalty to you, Dr. Rossey will be long gone as staff members either request transfers, retire, or work on automatic as they try to get through the day."

"Unlike your decision to retire early, so you could be healthy, write books, and enjoy what was left of the rest of your life, Mr. Davis will often come to work despite being sick because he won't want to lose any sick days for which he will be paid when he retires. But his health will become so bad that the school nurse will beg him to take a leave of absence."

Riley has seen and heard enough.

At that point, Mr. Helper sat down with Riley and told him the plan of the principals in Heaven.

"Riley, we are going to select one of our former principals to take Mr. Davis's identity. We will put that person into James' body until the school is returned to its elite status."

The board went through the process of interviewing candidates for the unique position. Although not super interested, Riley allowed himself to be a candidate and was promised something special as a reward if he was appointed. "Riley, I promise you if we select you to fulfill this important duty, you will receive the greatest reward we can possibly give." Riley thought about the potential appointment, knowing that going back as Mr. Davis would be a struggle.

Riley was interviewed, and the board reviewed his past accomplishments. Two other principals who also had great credentials were also interviewed. But Riley was the unanimous choice.

Mr. Helper began his work. First, he took a trip to Mr. Davis's hospital bed to make sure that all of his health problems were fixed without the awareness of the nurses. Then, after Riley was given very specific instructions on how to enter Davis's body, they are ready to proceed.

On their normal schedule of rounds, the nurses came into the room and were surprised at how great Mr. Davis looked. The new James had disconnected all the medical devices, and Mr. Helper had made sure all the power was off. "Excuse me, nurse, I have to go to the bathroom." The doctors were immediately called in. Just thirty minutes prior, the doctors thought there was a fifty percent chance that Mr. Davis wouldn't survive, but now all his vital signs are excellent.

Mr. Davis, alias Dr. Rossey, had gotten excited about his new mission and couldn't wait to return to the school. He was released in perfect health. The big question was, how would he react to the staff and students?

Dr. Rossey had his work cut out for him as he proceeded in Mr. Davis's body. Putting the school back on the road to success had become his new adventure and challenge.

Chapter 54

SENDING DR. ROSSEY BACK TO DR. RILEY ROSSEY HS

D r. Rossey knew this was a great opportunity. He also understood that he would not get another opportunity if he failed, and the reward awaiting him would not be his.

Riley returned on Monday with refreshments to thank his two assistants, four secretaries, and administrative assistants for all their hard work. This was not like Mr. Davis at all. Before they could say thank you, he said, "I'm off to walk the school and meet the teachers and students."

He was out of the office for hours as people welcomed him back. Some of his supporters remarked that they appreciated how he was greeting the staff and students. He was all in for lunch duties, hall duties, and visiting classrooms throughout the building.

"Maybe his illness brought him back to reality and changed him forever," said a teacher.

The task of confronting students and adults would be challenging as Mr. Davis was very good at being mad for no reason. He never answered questions and changed his mind more often than the tide turned.

Riley's pictures and awards around the school had always been an eyesore for Mr. Davis. As a matter of fact, one of the staff members had heard a rumor that Mr. Davis had considered planting a leak from the top floor to ruin all of Dr. Rossey's awards and pictures, but he decided not to because the cost of repairing the building would eat into his salary and pension, both of which had always been his main priority.

During Riley's first week as Mr. Davis, the staff actually began to feel as if their principal had been reborn. To keep his sanity, Riley wrote in a private diary about all he had been through: from being a bullied kid, to a model student, to a student favorite (and auto technician and computer expert), to a college success, to a great teacher, to a legendary administrator.

Dr. Rossey restarted an old tradition by sending staff to conferences instead of going himself. By having his assistants attend meetings, they began to grow and take ownership of where the school was headed.

Riley's day was reminiscent of how he had run the school for years. He began at six in the morning, about two and a half hours earlier than Mr. Davis had, and he was in the building usually till six at night, about three hours longer than Mr. Davis.

It didn't take long for the superintendent to call.

"Mr. Davis? Why have you changed your hours?"

"Well, I can't get done what I need to if I'm here only during class hours. I'm out of the office most of the day working with the students, and I need to make calls at night." Riley usually did that between seven and eight at night.

One night, the memory of Betzy Lejourner came to Riley's mind. *I wonder what happened to her. I would love to know since we left on such a sour note.* They had looked like they were going to make it as a couple, but the argument about class rank and Mr. Davis's actions had put a stop to that.

As Riley put his signature back on the school little by little, Mr. Helper often visited him to offer assistance. "You know, Riley, there are still people who think there were better candidates than you to take over for Mr. Davis. But most of us think you are making really good progress."

Riley sent a questionnaire to parents, students, staff, former graduates, and community members—including police and concerned citizens. He wanted to find out how others thought he was doing. The answers were a reflection of the past—some acknowledging long-overdue changes.

To Riley's shock, he received more than an eighty percent return of surveys, with most addressing negative aspects of the real Mr. Davis. Riley, being in Mr. Davis's body, found those comments difficult to respond to. He promised to institute a plan to address the input, which many did not believe. Some people did not put their names on the survey, but to those who did, Riley sent a letter asking for a face-to-face meeting or phone call. To Riley's surprise, that worked, too.

He also consulted with every group that had a stake in the school. That was certainly not Mr. Davis's usual way, whose modus operandi was to make his call and then be done. The fact that "Mr. Davis" was now interested in what others had to say surprised everyone. He had asked even those he had typically over-looked to complete the questionnaire: bus drivers, cafeteria workers, maintenance workers, and crossing guards. Even some vendors who had dealt with the school for years were included. The word circulated that Mr. Davis's health issues had really changed him.

Here were some of the concerns, most of which had been problems for the past two years but were never addressed by the real Mr. James:

1. Inconsistencies
2. Suspensions
3. Counseling services
4. Bathrooms
5. Playing favorites
6. Teachers not updating skills
7. Cafeteria problems
8. Favoritism of athletes
9. Student tardies and absences
10. Dress code violations
11. Teachers involved in inappropriate relationships
12. Administrators being in their offices too much
13. Discrimination against certain students
14. Teachers not knowing when to retire
15. Lack of communication with parents
16. Unnecessary and incessant memos
17. Threatening letters addressed to staff and parents

And the biggest issue that came up repeatedly on nearly every survey...

18. The ongoing bullying of students, teachers, and all other staff from the administration

To everyone's surprise, all the concerns and questions were addressed face to face, satisfying the staff. Although it took a full school year, under Riley's guidance, the school was beginning to get back on the right track.

Chapter 55

THE REAL MR. DAVIS IS GIVEN A CHANCE TO RETURN

When the school year was over, Riley was asked to return to Principal Heaven. He had saved the school, and it was time for Mr. Davis to go back into his own body and continue what was started by Dr. Rossey.

When Mr. Davis realized he had been resting comfortably for the past year in Heaven after contracting a serious illness, he was shocked. He was also surprised to learn that someone had been in his body during that time. He did not know that it was Riley Rossey or that Riley had set the school on a new track. Mr. Davis was instructed, however, that upon returning to his body, he must follow the plan of the person who had taken over his body and the school.

"If you do not follow this plan, you will come back to this Board, and we will consider revoking your pension and all the other benefits you are entitled to."

For James to hear that his money would be affected was enough for him to vow that he would run a good school. Of course, he thought he was a great principal and would have no problems.

Dr. Rossey had a chance to listen to the meeting between the Board and Mr. Davis. Riley couldn't believe his ears and knew this arrangement had very little chance of working. Since Riley had changed the school's trajectory, James would have to figure out how to get by with very little personal investment. He didn't realize that many had considered the "old Mr. Davis" a political failure.

As James entered the school for the first time, he immediately noticed the building was immaculate. It was summer, and he arrived just fifteen minutes before the staff, nearly two hours later than Riley would have. The staff gave him a great welcome, and his assistants wasted no time before sharing information with him.

Betty Juneton entered Mr. Davis's office to give him five messages that had already been left early that morning. He automatically read them and responded by telling her who should handle the calls. She wondered if her boss was having a problem.

"Are you okay, James?"

"Of course. I am fine, Mrs. Juneton," he answered shortly, surprised she had called him by his first name.

Betty walked away, a little puzzled. Why was he addressing her so formally, and why was he acting so hands-off? James went into his office, shut the door, and reminded himself that he had to act right or he would lose his pension.

The conniving bully-extraordinaire walked back out of his office and was nice as can be.

As time went by, Mr. Davis began to think that whoever had taken over the school had brainwashed the staff, students, the board of education, and the community. The school that James left was no longer the same. The staff, parents, and students had been the decision-makers, but now things ran smoothly, and protocols were followed. Most notably, the staff now worked together, and everyone seemed productive and happy.

James tried to find the name of the last principal, but everyone looked at him like he was crazy. "What are you talking about? Of course, Dr. Riley Rossey was the principal before you, but that was years ago."

Riley, with his fourteen-hour days and visionary plan, had made the staff happy and the school run well. And, although the Board ensured that James' body was at full strength so he could continue the work Riley started, it took him less than a week to realize that this job was not for him. He signaled the Board and asked to go to Heaven over the weekend. "Listen, this is much more work than any one person can handle. How many people worked this job while I was laid up?"

"Just one," Mr. Helper responded. "You know the deal. If you don't do the job as planned, you will die, losing your pension and health benefits, of course."

James recognized he was in a bind, so he began to think about the changes he must make to stay in the program. He decided that the name of the game was to keep your mouth shut, be a yes-man, and make sure everyone was happy.

With the loss of his life and pension loss staring him in the face, James struggled. He no longer desired to be the principal of the school. After just a few weeks, he began falling back into his old habits, but was careful to make sure his inattentiveness to details went unnoticed.

Those off-campus Friday meetings that the other staff had been encouraged to attend? James decided to attend those himself, giving him extra time away from the school. He cut corners by responding to issues via email rather than having in-person meetings. And he even canceled the regularly scheduled weekly staff meetings, because they fell on Friday.

Additionally, James set out to pad his own pockets. He cut expenses by not purchasing new uniforms for various athletic teams and limiting teachers' expense accounts. He also changed the previously approved budget numbers for numerous programs, allocating funds differently.

The staff who found out about these things were baffled and disappointed. He told them that anyone who would like to discuss these adjustments could email him, and he would set up an appointment to discuss their concerns. Of course, he never answered any of those emails. His excuse was that his computer began acting up, so he would get back to email another day. But that day never came.

Despite cutting all these corners, James could not handle his expected daily schedule. It didn't take long for him to slide entirely back into his old ways. Some of his old cronies began to say they wanted the old James back.

Chapter 56

THE FINAL CONFRONTATION

Riley, now the chairperson for Principal Heaven, thought there might have been a very slight chance for James to change, but it became crystal clear that would never happen. Davis's bullying and lazy habits had been fully exposed. He had not lived up to his agreement. Of course, James had no idea that Riley was the spokesperson for the Principal Heaven group.

The group agreed to bring James back to Heaven. And one weekend, Mr. Helper made sure that this happened. James was shocked when Mr. Helper showed up at his house. "Those in Principal Heaven would like to speak to you."

James, being the ever-defensive person, argued that he was doing his part as agreed. But Mr. Helper saw things for what they were, and James was brought to the conference room in Principal Heaven. He sat waiting to hear from the group. Of course, he could only hear voices, except for the chairperson, who entered the room with a hooded robe.

The main question presented was, "Why are we seeing the old Mr. Davis?"

The group reviewed James' life, from his birth to the present day. The committee told James that they knew his father was very abusive, and they knew he felt that abuse even throughout his stay inside his mom.

"Your turmoil was constant throughout your life; you became a liar, a bully, and a person focused only on your own satisfaction. But we gave you an opportunity to change, and you refused to do so." A video of his life then appeared before him—all the miserable chapters in James' life flashed by, narrated by Dr. Rossey. Victims of his bullying, lying, deception, and abuse were highlighted.

When the video finished playing, Riley entered the room and removed the hood from his head. James nearly had a heart attack; he was shaking and trembling.

Riley said, "Do you have anything to say before I give you the Board's decision on your future?"

James was too shaken to say or do anything.

"Well, James, the Board has decided that you will fall ill and will officially die. A new principal will take your place."

James screamed out, "What about my pension and my vacation days? I put in my time. This is a kangaroo court!"

"You will be given one more chance. You will be reborn and experience a quiet childhood. If you follow the right path and treat people as they should be, you will work as an adult for thirty years, and then you will enjoy your pension."

"WHAT? You're telling me, in my seventies, that I will have to be reborn and work for thirty more years before I can collect my pension? That's not fair."

The Board members see that James does not get it, nor will he ever get it.

"You win, Dr. Rossey," James mumbled.

Riley replied, "I win nothing. The thousands of people you came in contact with will win. Your thirty years of upcoming work will decide the next thirty years. If, for some reason, that doesn't work, the court will again determine how you will die."

"Why can't I just be in Principal Heaven like everyone else?"

"Because you are not like everyone else. Many have suffered at your hand since you were born, but now you have a chance to make up for it."

Chapter 57

EPILOGUE

Riley did receive his reward from the angels—he got to see his dad and his grandpa in heaven. They spent countless hours together, talking about their pasts and how they were able to affect so many lives. But Riley's reward did not end there.

Riley was told to sit in a room while his final award would be coming to say hello. As he waited patiently, in walked Betzy Lejourner, looking as beautiful as ever. Riley nearly fainted. But instead, he quickly ran to her, and they hugged and kissed.

"Why are you in Principal Heaven?"

Betzy explained, "When I went away to college, I felt so bad about you and me. As the days went by, I decided to change my major to education. I taught preschool for many years; then I became a director before taking a position at an elementary school as a principal. Unfortunately, I became ill and had to retire early. Because I had such an impact on kids, I was rewarded with Principal Heaven."

Riley was stunned. The two can't take their eyes off each other. Betzy said, "I stayed in Arizona."

"Did you ever get married or have children?"

"No, I was always too busy with school and college and just got lost in time," she responded to Riley.

For Riley and Betzy, this was definitely a match in heaven. Each day was a blessing as they spent time together. Their closeness became love, and the love became permanent.

Riley, his dad, grandpa, and Betzy shared so much about their lives as school leaders. They wrote several books for other students who were bullied and changed hundreds of lives. Somehow, the books found their way to the schools on earth, thanks to Mr. Helper. The four leaders became very special writers.

Word of Mr. Davis's death spread. At his funeral, family members thanked everyone for coming, and as the church ceremony came to a close, Jon, who spent his whole life in and out of trouble with the law, said, "I wish Uncle James would have been a better role model for me and others. I guess the only thing I learned from him was how to be a bully and a lousy son."

Later, Jon talked to the Reverend Slipdiss, who became a new role model for him. Jon, learning you are never too old to make the right decision, decided to follow God, and found his new path in life. The first person he counseled was John Plasner, who had also led a tough life, living out his days in jail.

Chapter 58

REMEMBERING DR. ROSSEY

A new principal was selected to lead the Mason School District's high school. He had been a student mentored by Dr. Rossey. On his first day, he paid tribute to the new class and unveiled a plaque that said, "Dr. Riley Rossey, Your memory will remain in our hearts as the greatest bully fighter of all time. You spent your life making students, teachers, school staff, and parents better."

Mr. Alfred, who had lived a long life, regularly placed fresh flowers beside the plaque in memory of his friend, the best mentee and mentor of all time. He enjoys each day, fishing and guiding maintenance and custodial staff, who carefully and lovingly maintain and care for Dr. Riley Rossey High School.

Appendix

What Educational Leadership Books Don't Tell You to Remember

After reading Riley's story, you may wonder, does everything you read in books happen? Although his story is fictional, during my 38 years in the public educational system—27 as a school administrator—I have been a live witness to many situations similar to the occurrences I wrote about. Being an administrator puts you at the forefront of everything that happens in the school system.

With that in mind, for your reference, I wanted to add these 100 points that educational leadership books don't tell you to remember. I hope they will help you if you are navigating the education system as a teacher or administrator and give you wisdom into what can and should be in a school system if you are a parent or student. If you want one single takeaway, my best tip is always to say what you mean and mean what you say.

1. Take care of problems immediately, especially from parents.

2. Making mistakes is okay; not immediately correcting them allows them to grow into bigger problems.

3. Don't blow off a kid when he wants to talk to you. That same kid may be a danger to himself or others.

4. If the politics at a school are too much, start looking for a new job. You are there for the kids; don't forget it.

5. Report abuse immediately. Don't worry about the effects of giving your name—it's confidential.

6. Get that bully issue settled immediately; put them in the corner they deserve to be in.

7. Stop beating up teachers and parents with calls and memos; you may be beaten back.

8. If you need to talk honestly with bad teachers, do it. Determine if you need another staff member present with you.

9. Be aggressive, not passive. Kids and parents don't like wimps. You are not there to be popular but respected.

10. Be positive even in the most negative situations.

11. Stop worrying that a teacher is your friend. Supervise them.

12. Who is paying your bills? Do the job they require.

13. Think before you say something stupid to a kid.

14. Your students are not your peers.

15. Be careful what you say outside the shop about the shop.

16. Volunteer; stop worrying about how much time it takes.

17. If you need a second job, make it your second job.

18. Female or male relationship with staff is a big NO.

19. Don't be an office rat. Go where the kids are.

20. Being early is on time; being on time is late.

21. Dress appropriately, despite what others do.

22. Walk through the building early and during the day.

23. Communicate with staff live, face to face.

24. Ride a school bus occasionally, both before and after school.

25. Show up for minor events as well as major events.

26. Treat free time as a look-and-see; walk and talk.

27. Unless demanded, all written reports come after kids.

28. Listen with two ears, talk with one mouth.

29. Let students have input into dressing up the school.

30. Define input; it does not mean that people get their way.

31. Encourage student ideas to improve learning.

32. Misconduct reports should be short and to the point.

33. Don't curse or be mean.

34. Mental health days are Saturday and Sunday.

35. Make sure challenged kids have the best teachers.

36. Hire a diverse population, but always hire the best candidates.

37. Make sure athletics are about more than the superstars.

38. Weekends and nights are not off-limits for those who work in the school system.

39. Consult with past employees for their input if needed.

40. Have a strong and active parent group. Define their role.

41. Some board members are only "wanna-be's." Be careful.

42. Consistency and follow-up is not just for top parents.

43. Pick the best candidate. Let your superior disagree.

44. Don't be afraid to report abusive parents.

45. Inspect your building early in the day.

46. You need student, employee, and parent snitches.

47. Know what your building hot spots are.

48. Attend events in individual classes when invited.

49. Do not assume (ass u me) anything.

50. Kids come as is; they pay your salary.

51. Train your assistants. Don't fear them taking your job.

52. Have close relationships with police and other officials.

53. Help and assist teachers who want your job.

54. Invite community members to events.

55. Treat your paraprofessionals like gold.

56. Don't have unnecessary meetings or overuse memos.

57. Make your office teacher- and student-friendly.

58. Don't touch kids unnecessarily; you never know.

59. Regular parents rate as high as influential parents.

60. Make modifications and adjustments as needed.

61. If the job were easy, everyone would do it.

62. Make security a high priority.

63. Keep in touch with and welcome past students.

64. Check out your bus area, street lights, and signs.

65. Your best students and athletes should be role models.

66. Sit with students who may be looked at as strange.

67. Never promise without delivering.

68. Follow and promote the 24-hour rule for parent contact.

69. Check guest speakers. The kids will get even if they stink.

70. Keep your personal problems to yourself or your superiors.

71. Student meetings should never be canceled.

72. Make sure employees receive proper training before having kid contact.

73. Check emergency doors frequently.

74. Visibility is a must in the building. Keep stressing it.

75. Parent meetings should be canceled for emergencies only.

76. Stress staff health; you need to be a role model.

77. Select teachers as your eyes and ears. Watch details.

78. Promote random acts of kindness.

79. Remember kid's names. They respect that.

80. Separate friendship from supervising.

81. Teachers' duties need to be a joint effort.

82. Drivers outside of the building need to be monitored.

83. Check emergency exits regularly to ensure they are working.

84. Safety equipment is important for staff and students.

85. Nurses and counselors need to roam the building.

86. Write reports on time (after the kids leave).

87. Supervise the cafeteria, gym, hallways, and student commons.

88. Stress an open-door policy with appointments.

89. Some teachers always welcome visitors.

90. Have an annex office in hot spots.

91. Distribute job descriptions. Define them if necessary.

92. Respect unions and associations, but know they don't run you.

93. Send different people to in- and out-of-district meetings.

94. Don't send unnecessary group memos to people who are doing their job.

95. Have assigned staff visit seriously hurting kids at homes.

96. Clean graffiti immediately; check with snitches for those responsible.

97. Limit student handbook and teacher handbook pages.

98. Keep up to date on other administration resources.

99. Don't lie to students; they want to be able to trust you.

100. Give compensatory time to employees when earned.

In Memory of Miss Dorothy Gould

This book has been written with the two best principals and administrators this author has ever seen in the past forty-plus years in mind. So, who were these two people?

Dorothy Gould, as remembered by her long-time caretaker Michalene Bowman: Dorothy Gould was a unique individual—an individual whose own soul and vision manifest in rare strength, uncompromising integrity, and a deep love for her fellow humans. This legendary lady has never ceased struggling with strength, honesty, and care for the youth of Newark, New Jersey.

Refusing to flee through the bad times, Dorothy remained in her city. She was a product of the Newark School System, entering kindergarten at Charlton Street School and graduating from South Side High School, now called Shabazz High School. She attended Upsala College in East Orange, majoring in mathematics and English. She applied to the Newark Board of Education for a teaching job and, in 1943, became the first Afro-American teacher at Cleveland Junior High School in Newark, New Jersey.

While teaching, she realized the importance of education for kids to succeed. She continued her education at Montclair State College and received her Master of Arts degree in 1950. She was offered a job in the Montgomery Boys Pre-Vocational School. Again working with her students, she completed her certification in special education from Newark State College, now Kean University. She continued teaching at Montgomery Pre Vocational School for thirteen years and then became the principal, shaping the school into an exceptional education facility.

In 1982, Dorothy Gould became Assistant Executive Superintendent for Pupil Personnel Services at the Board of Education office in Newark. She was responsible for the building and implementation of the New Jersey Regional Day School for multiple handicapped students. The school was later recognized as one of the best day schools for multiple handicapped students in New Jersey.

Following her retirement after 43 years of service, she was recruited by Dean Dillard Robinson of Trinity Saint Philips Academy to be part of a very special project.

Dorothy was dismayed by the inequality of education in the inner-city schools. In 1988, The Centennial House at 2 Park Place in the heart of Newark was identified for this special project—St. Phillips Academy, an independent school founded in the Episcopal tradition. She was a founding board member and recognized as a member emeritus.

"Dot," as she was known by her closest friends, had a total commitment to her profession. Her integrity and unflinching insistence that all students, teachers, and administrators alike give their utmost for the purpose of learning came to be known throughout the city. Dot said, "You must be accountable for all of this, not only with self-assurance, but with humor and complete lack of pretense." She did not forget her roots and indeed drew nourishment from them. She used her talent of relating to people regardless of age, race, social or economic status to focus on promoting the greater good, not only in the field of education but in community service as well.

Dorothy never stopped giving. For many years, she served on the Board of Friendly Fuld Neighborhood House, Girl Scouts Council of Greater Essex County. With twenty-five years as a scout leader and with the N.A.A.C.P. and Y. M.C.A., she was initiated into the Sigma Theta Society North Alumnae Chapter in 1949. She served in the North Jersey Chapter from 1954-1958.

In December 2001, during PAC's Kwanza Honoree Celebration, she was recognized as one of Newark's Outstanding Community Elders. Dot was a long-standing member of Trinity Saint Phillips Episcopal Cathedral Parish in Newark.

Dorothy continued giving to herself without measure to her high ideals in education and community services. She continued to forge ahead, accomplishing goals and overcoming obstacles. She was one whose love and loyalty for Newark is exceeded only by the young who dwell within it.

At the tender age of 90, she continued to receive calls for advice and voiced her opinion on challenges faced by many individuals. Often, it was from several people who were decades her junior. Hearing her strength, you would be among many who were just in awe of her. Mention a family name or event from the history of Newark, and she had a story to share.

On May 31, 2015, this one-of-a-kind lady passed away at the age of 93.

About Dorothy Gould, as told by Robert Fishbein

I remember the first day I met Miss Dorothy Gould, in May 1969. It was the strangest way to meet someone who would influence and change my life. I was leaving from New Jersey to Fort Lauderdale, Florida. I was scheduled to take the CPA exam and was getting my last spring break vacation in before entering the real world.

During my drive to Florida with a college friend, we got lost as Route 95 was not entirely built, and we kept taking side roads. We wound up at a Howard Johnson restaurant in North Carolina. During a trip to the men's room, I met a man from New Jersey who asked me where we were going. It turned out we were actually heading back toward New Jersey due to the confusing roadways. He directed us back to the south toward Florida.

After some small talk, the man said he was a teacher and councilman in Newark and talked me into meeting the principal at Alyea Street School, since the principal needed substitute teachers during the end of the school year. *Okay,* I thought to myself, *I'll get an emergency certificate and make a few bucks before taking the CPA test.*

When I called, the building secretary told me I would be meeting with the principal, Miss Dorothy Gould. I arrived and went into her office, noticing the three-ring sign for a popular beer outside her window. She then told me she had recently hired staff and would be okay, but one of the nearby schools was desperate for substitutes. She made a phone call and said these exact words, "I have a nut who wants to work in your school."

The man on the other end of the line said, "Send him over."

The principal was my junior high counselor. When I entered his office, he was facing the wall and started to speak to me. I knew this was not a good sign. The school under his watch was a central school for all the most disruptive kids in Newark schools. I spent two months there, and despite some crazy days, I enjoyed it. The school cafeteria was like a daily war zone. I ran out of clean shirts and ties really quickly.

My father had a business in Newark, and some of the kids knew me from my first day as a substitute teacher. Others knew me from playing basketball in the playgrounds of Newark.

I knew the principal was not long for the school. I was told he was not only burnt out but on the way to retirement.

Then, the unexpected happened. Dorothy Gould became principal at this school and asked me if I would like to teach there in September since I was getting good reviews. I left the CPA test and more than twice the money on the table. Why? Two words: Dorothy Gould.

It did not take long for Dorothy to straighten out the school and make it look like a school should look. She quickly changed attitudes and perceptions, basically saying get out of here if you're not interested in working hard. She then began to pick her staff. She kept the teachers who wanted to be part of the exciting changes and helped those not interested find a new career. She was like the general manager of a sports team. She was finding new homes, even for the most experienced people, or forcing them to retire.

The people who stayed knew she would not accept anything but the best. Dot knew many of the students were very intelligent and needed someone to encourage, teach, and make them feel like they were exceptional students. They were not emotionally disturbed children but exceptional special education students, of which many were classified.

Well, she got to me. I changed majors, returning to school to get a special education degree. For all intents and purposes she became my instant mentor. Even after I left that school four years later for a larger school, Dorothy and I remained close. Over the years, I called her for advice to learn more about teaching and supervision. And I always called her on her birthday, Mother's Day, Easter, Christmas, and usually two other times a month.

I met many of her family members at family functions and was honored to sit at the family table at her retirement. She was honored by every important politician in Newark as well as government officials in New Jersey. It was difficult not to find staff members who wanted to work for Dorothy.

After I relocated to Florida, I came to New Jersey for a fundraiser every April starting in 2004. I made it a point to visit her. We always talked about her educational experiences, and she always answered my questions and concerns, even when she was ninety years of age.

The two main rules she always followed were: "Don't mess with my kids," and "Kids come as is." Dorothy had very little use for politicians but knew she had to keep them happy. Unless they were vested in kids, she really had nothing to say to them. The last time I saw Dorothy was April 2015. Her caretaker stood there in disbelief as she was supposed to be incoherent and blind. But somehow, I was able to communicate with her. She even laughed as we joked about some of our experiences. Our last words were, "I love you." I believe I was one of the last professionals who was able to say goodbye in person.

Dorothy had a seventy-year career, working informally for twenty-three years in education. I remember bringing my daughter to meet her. My daughter was blown away by her advice, standards, and how she remembered all I had told her about our family.

Dorothy's caretaker was phenomenal. Michalene had been one of her Brownie Scouts who had never forgotten Dorothy. Dorothy lived by one standard as a principal, best described by Jimmy Brown in one of his movies: "I'm not the white sheriff; I'm not the black sheriff. I'm the SHERIFF."

I loved Dot, and I thank her for steering me in the right direction. You can find hundreds and hundreds of people who would say the same thing about her.

In Memory of Dr. William "Mickey" Harvey

In the Words of His Beloved Wife Gerri Harvey

Dr. Harvey was born in Aberdeen, Maryland. He obtained his B.S. degree from the University of Maryland. Dr. Harvey completed his doctorate requirements at Rutgers University in New Jersey. His education at Carver Vocational Technical High School in Baltimore gave us more ammunition to show that vocational students can be successful in college.

Dr. Harvey had a distinguished 25-year career in urban and suburban districts servicing multi-cultured and multi-racial populations. He was recruited from graduate school to become an assistant professor at Newark State College, now Kean University. He was then recruited to the Newark Public Schools by his beloved mentor, Dorothy Gould. He held administrative positions, including the industrial arts director, Director of Student Personnel Services, Principal Assistant Superintendent of Schools, Executive Superintendent of Schools, and Superintendent of Schools.

His many accomplishments did not go unnoticed. He was the recipient of the Northern New Jersey Tuskegee Alumni Education Award, Newark Technical Leadership Award, Essex County Leadership Award, Safe Haven Community Service Award, City of Plainfield Charles Allen Community Service Award, and Plainfield Ebony Association Award.

"Mickey" or "Harvey," as his friends and family called him, enjoyed his life and had a personal relationship with God. Many lifelong friends and extended family members were very important to him.

His photography hobby yielded a lifelong collage of pictures and "this is your life" moments. He loved his cars and trucks, having learned his trade at vocational school, and was always able to diagnose auto problems with his advanced training skills. He enjoyed taking pictures on trips with his family and friends. He had holiday gatherings at his homes in Scotch Plains, Plainfield, while vacationing in the Poconos. He found his trips to Europe and his cruises enjoyable.

First and foremost, he was a family man devoted to his children and wife. His three children were his lifeline, and he was theirs. He was one of a kind, and his memory will live on forever.

As told by Robert Fishbein

It's funny how it didn't matter to Mickey whether he hired a male, female, veteran teacher, or a new teacher. It came down to the best candidate. He knew the kids he was hiring the teacher to teach. He was most concerned that the teachers were technically sound and they had the skills, particularly in the vocational-technical schools where we worked. He would not be comfortable if we had to hire people who were forced on him just because they knew somebody to get hired. That was called a political appointee and was not Mickey's style.

Dr. Harvey worked his way to Montgomery School almost by accident. Maybe that is where we were similar. He was teaching at Newark State College, and several teachers were assigned to Montgomery for student teaching, with Mickey as their supervising teacher. Meanwhile, we met in a very strange way. He was carrying an out-of-control student over his shoulder in the cafeteria when he approached me and said, "Hi, my name is Mickey Harvey."

It seemed that Mickey was entrenched as a professor at the college, but it did not take long for Miss Gould to convince him to work at Montgomery.

Coincidentally, since the supervisor of what was called Industrial Arts at the time was retiring, Mickey was appointed to follow the retiring supervisor around to see if it was a good fit. You bet it was a good fit. Mickey found out quickly that it does not get any better than working for Dorothy Gould. By examining several depleted programs with out-of-date equipment, Mickey found and wrote grants to purchase up-to-date equipment and supplies. His main objective was to make the students employable with what they would find in business.

During my teaching experience, the school accounting person became ill, and there was no one to watch the shops purchase of supplies for their programs. Since I had the background, Dorothy pulled me out to work with Mickey, and we became instant friends. Mickey went back to the college and raved about Montgomery to his students. He was able to bring in top-shelf students, and he took care of the discipline problems along with Dorothy. Mickey was the worst when it came to politics, only surpassed by Dorothy.

The kids we had there were supposedly the worst-behaved kids in Newark, and Montgomery was the central drop-off point or school of last resort. It did not work that way for Mickey. He ran the shop as a training program for getting jobs and even recruited employers who wanted to teach their trade.

The maintenance and custodial kitchen help and security learned the party was over. The school was going to be run like any other high school. Dorothy was an expert at having the effective teachers chase the ineffective teachers out, and she taught that to Mickey.

Since Dorothy lived in Newark, she took everything and treated it like her own. She treated the kids like they were her own. Mickey had more time to work with the students since the students stayed at Montgomery longer. Many stayed back and had a few extra years to learn from Mickey and their teachers.

Mickey's brilliance and creativity extended to grant writing and getting the school much-needed equipment. It seemed that all the teachers Dorothy and Mickey interviewed accepted the jobs because of them.

Mickey's schedule was very hectic at first, to say the least. I almost wondered if I was going to be drawn into his schedule: work through the week, visit and take care of his family in Baltimore on weekends, return to his wife, write grants and more grants. He was a great father and husband.

After working and teaching others at Montgomery, Mickey took a job at Somerset County Vocational School. I was already in my new district, and he made sure I followed him to Somerset two years later. There, we worked together to build great programs. The person who left had to do what Mickey did in Montgomery to bring the school up-to-date with equipment and supplies. I learned more about special education and how students need to be taught. In the process, our families and Dorothy's family had become lifelong friends.

People who knew Mickey and his wife, Gerri, knew about their integrity and love of people, regardless of age, race, or religion.

One of the several stories that describe Mickey and Gerri was when their neighbor's house burnt down next door to their home. They welcomed the family, including their teenage son, to live in their home until they could rebuild their home, no matter how long it took. Rose, Gallie, and Tommy are still part of the Harvey family.

Mickey's passing while still in the prime of his life was shocking. To Dorothy, Mickey was the son she never had. To me, he was the big brother I never had.

I'm sure Mickey would like to know how to get education to work without political interference. If he is talking to Dorothy in heaven, I'm sure they are both still working to make education and life a better experience for others.

About the Author

Bob Fishbein is a retired middle and high school Teacher, Director of Student Services, Assistant Baseball Coach, Softball Coach, Director of Support Services, District Supervisor of Special Services, Adjunct University Professor, and Assistant Principal/Principal of Special Needs, Guidance Counselor, Middle and High School Basketball Referee, and Stop Smoking Cessation Counselor, with over thirty-eight years' experience in six counties in New Jersey and two counties in Florida, in urban, suburban and rural counties, in both comprehensive and vocational schools.

Bob was raised in and graduated from the K-12 schools in Newark, New Jersey. He has published three other books. *Inspired by a Promise, If You Decide Your Wish is Your Command, A Journey to Stop Smoking Forever*, and *Senior Snowbird and the School Teacher*. He was honored by three governors in New Jersey for grants he wrote for several million dollars.

Bob wrote this book to point out to teachers how amazing they are and applaud them for the great impact they have on students.

Bob and Betz, his supportive wife, have three adult children—two who are married, four grandchildren, and numerous nieces, nephews, and godchildren between them. His late wife, Debby, was always a positive inspiration.

A special thanks to Mr. Alfred Stevens, one of the best friends anyone could ever pray for, and to Mrs. Harvey, Mickey's wife, Craig, Crystal, William, and the best children and grandchildren a family could ask for. To Michalene, thank you for keeping Dorothy healthy all those years and being a Godsend to her children and extended family. To Jennifer Jones, thank you for your proofreading expertise.

Mickey Harvey, Dot Gould, and Bob Fishbein working at
Montgomery Pre-Vocational School, Newark, New Jersey, in the 1970s.